VIRTUAL MAGIC

ACADEMY OF MODERN MAGIC, BOOK 2

MAGGIE ALABASTER

To Courtney, Margo, Kim, KD, Cath, Sarah, Katie and Loraine for your support during some hard times. And to anyone else I've forgotten to thank!

"You are *not* going back there."

My mother's face was an interesting shade of blotchy pink. Not cute like Kane when he blushed, but uneven like her voice when she spoke to me.

I tossed a shoe into my bag. "Of course I am. Well —" I stood up straight and toyed with my hair for a moment. "I'm not exactly going back. The Academy of Modern Magic has moved to another campus."

"I'm well aware of that." Lucinda Knight-Chapel gave me a look which would have reduced most other people, paranormal or otherwise, to a blubbering mess at her feet. Probably not literally, though who knows. Others seemed to find her intimidating.

As for me, I shrugged off the look and searched for my other shoe. "Are you trying to say the University of Arcana campus isn't safe?" I shot her a challenging look. She had gone there herself. Not only that, She had been fifteen when she graduated. Surely I should get bonus points for stepping foot on a campus where she was all but revered? To be honest, I would rather put my head in a blender, but after the Zeta attack, the academy needed to be moved. Apparently, the university was the safest place for us. Besides, my lovers and my best friend would be going.

"Of course it's safe," she snapped. That was followed by a deep sigh. You know, the kind mothers do when their children refuse to listen. "I just want you to be careful and not get harmed. Is that such a terrible thing?"

Now *I* sighed. The kind daughters do when their mothers are being, well, motherly, but the daughter is nineteen and wants to make her own mistakes.

I flopped down on my bed. "I know you're just worried about me, but I can look after myself, remember? The best place I can be is where I can learn more about using my magic."

She perched beside me. "You shouldn't have to

look after yourself. They came after you because of me."

"They" were Zeta. A more or less secret government organisation, whose goal it was to bring normals and paranormals under their heel. Part of that meant taking witches like me and using us to create hybrids—witch and shifter cross. None of that was part of my life plan.

"They would have come after the whole academy sooner or later," I reminded her. "Me being there was probably a coincidence." Except I knew it wasn't. My best friend Ariana and my friend-cum-nemesis, Matt, had been told to protect me. Even my lover and teacher, Nash, was supposed to be keeping an eye on me. Just thinking about seeing him again made my heart race.

My mother eyed me. "Peyton, even if it was a coincidence, I wouldn't want you to go back there."

"How else am I going to learn how to use magic better?" I asked. "Do you have the time?"

She flinched. "I have to leave for North America in the morning. Your father—"

"Isn't as trained as you or my teachers are," I finished for her. I felt bad for saying that. I loved my father dearly, but he hardly bothered to use the power he had. It wasn't that he couldn't, but he never seemed interested. I never gave it much thought until now. From the look on my mother's face, neither had she.

"I will find someone—" she started, but was interrupted by the sound of the doorbell.

"It sounds like my escort has arrived." I rose and zipped up my suitcase.

I thought she might argue further, but she stood and gave me a hug. She didn't look happy in the slightest. She held a lot of power in the paranormal community. I knew full well she could have forbidden me from going back to school and no establishment would dare take me. If nothing else, her indifference had shaped me into the independent woman I was. I don't know if it was that indifference which led her to let me go now, or the knowledge I would never forgive her if she didn't.

Either way, she stepped aside to let me zip up my suitcase. I grabbed my backpack off my bed and headed downstairs.

Standing beside the door, face bright red, was Kane, one of my boyfriends and one of the sweetest guys I know. Beside him stood his brother, Dyson, the clown of the family. Twins—fraternal—were both shifters. Right now, however, they were both smiling, in spite of my father's scrutiny. He must have let them in.

"Hey," I greeted them. I handed my backpack to Dyson and gave both guys a warm embrace and a kiss on the mouth.

My father cleared his throat and gave me a funny look, but smiled. "Are you going to introduce me?'"

I gave him a please-don't-embarrass-me look and nodded. "This is Dyson and Kane Gill. They're both, um, friends of mine." Gods, what were they exactly? I was dating them both and sleeping with Kane. Dyson and I had agreed to take things slowly. I didn't know if any of that meant they were my boyfriends. I mean, who has two boyfriends anyway? Or three if you count Nash. I was definitely sleeping with him, too. The fact he was a teacher complicated things, but we made it work so far.

"This is my dad." I jerked a thumb toward him.

"Nice to meet you, sir." Dyson held out his hand and Kane followed suit shortly after.

"You too, boys." Dad shook their hands and gave them a nod.

I winced. *Boys*? I suppose they were to him.

"So," Dad went on, "you'll take good care of my little girl?"

I groaned. "Dad!" I drew the word out like a whiny child.

Dyson just grinned. "We'll take very good care of her, sir. She's in good hands with us."

I heard Kane swallow and had a pretty good idea where his thoughts had gone. We hadn't seen each other since just after Christmas and the dry spell after a couple of semesters of getting laid regularly… Let's just say my trusty vibrator got a workout.

"Yes." Kane's agreement came out as a squeak. "She'll be safe with us."

Dad blinked at him several times. "Well…good. See that she is, otherwise—"

"They know Mum will hunt them down and have them flayed alive," I assured him. I gave the guys a wink, which probably looked more like I was squinting with both eyes. Winking was never a skill I had mastered.

Dyson grinned. "I hope not. I'm attached to my skin." The mischievous look in his eyes made my heart skip a beat. I knew exactly which piece of skin he was referring to.

I resisted the urge to look in the direction of his dick.

He gave me an innocent look as if he knew what I was thinking.

"Anyway," I drew the word out, "we should get going. We have to beat the traffic."

"Yes, we do." Dyson took my backpack from my father and Kane grabbed the handle of my suitcase.

"Gentlemen, I see." Dad looked pleased.

I was perfectly capable of carrying and dragging my own things, but it gave me a chance to hug my dad and kiss his cheek.

"Stay out of trouble, little witch," he said affectionately.

I caught Dyson's smile and gave him a warning glare over Dad's shoulder. If he thought he'd use the term of endearment as a nickname, he had better think again.

He just smiled more broadly and stepped out into the cool of a Melbourne morning in March.

I followed both guys and closed the door behind me. Something about it felt final, although I knew I'd be back at the end of the year.

"New car?" I asked, eyeing the red Ford something-or-other. I am no expert on cars.

"It's Kane's," Dyson replied. "It matches his face."

"Hey!" Kane protested. "I didn't choose the colour."

"I'm sure you didn't," I assured him. "As long as it

goes..." I peered into the back as we got closer and groaned. "What is *he* doing here?"

Matt wound down the window and smirked back at me. "I'd say it's nice to see you too, but..." He shrugged.

I gave him the finger. Evidently we were going to start the academic year the way we'd left the last one.

He rolled his eyes and raised the window again.

"Officially, he's going the same way we are," Kane said. He opened the back of the car and lifted my suitcase inside.

"And unofficially?" I asked.

"He insisted," Dyson said, his hand cupped around his mouth as if that would stop Matt from being able to hear. "He was sure you'd get into some kind of trouble on the way there."

"You *know* she would," Matt called out.

I grimaced. "I would not." Trouble might find me, though. "Do I have to sit in the back with him?"

"Dyson gets carsick," Kane said regretfully. "And I'm driving, otherwise I'd sit in the back with you."

I knew what that meant. While the guys in front watched the road, he'd have his hands down my top and my shorts. No such luck sitting beside Matt.

I sighed loudly and pulled the door open. "Fine,

but no funny business." I shook my finger but I was mostly joking. Matt was a dick, but he was hot as hells, especially dressed from head to toe in black. His muscles bulged in a way that made my eyes pop. I would totally go there. Maybe.

He snorted. "Like that'll happen."

I slipped into the seat and stuck my tongue out at him. "Always the charmer."

"That's me," he agreed. "Now shut the door. You never know when we might come under attack."

I gave him a look, but closed the door quickly. Zeta could be waiting anywhere. I couldn't afford to let my guard down.

I hunkered down in the seat and clicked the belt into place. My father stood in the front window. I waved. He waved back. I saw no sign of my mother.

With a shrug I turned back around. "So, we're all second years."

"Yep," Dyson said. He kept the window down beside him, his face in the breeze. I wouldn't have been surprised if his tongue lolled out.

"It's remarkable you managed to survive first year," Matt said. A smile tugged at the corner of his mouth.

I gave him a sidelong look. "Is this where I say

thank you for saving my ass, or you're welcome because I saved yours?" I asked.

"Or where we remind him Nash saved us all by biting the head off a griffin." Dyson glanced over his shoulder.

"That was pretty cool," I said. Nash wouldn't agree. He had killed before and it haunted him. Doing it again…

I hated that I hadn't been able to talk to him since the bus picked us up at the academy. I hadn't seen or heard from him for weeks. With any luck, he would be at the combined university slash academy campus, waiting for us.

I sighed softly. If I called him a boyfriend then I was a pretty crap girlfriend. I had tried to contact him over the holidays, but I hadn't managed to reach him. I didn't know what number to call or what email to try. I had casually asked my mother about dragon shifters, but she had laughed it off. A high pitched, nervous laugh, to be sure, but I got no answers.

"As long as he can tell a good gargoyle from a bad one," Matt muttered.

I leaned over to pat his arm. "It's easy to tell. You were the one who was always getting injured."

He gave me a long look. "Only to keep you safe, remember?"

"I didn't say I didn't appreciate it," I told him. "I'm glad you're not dead and stuff."

"Gee, thanks," he said sarcastically.

"Um, guys," Kane said from the driver's seat. "We're being followed."

I SWIVELLED AROUND in my seat and looked out the back window. "How do you know?" I was looking for a black SUV with tinted windows, like the one my mother drove. Except, you know, driven by bad guys.

"That blue car has been behind us since we pulled out of your place," Kane said.

"It's a busy road," I pointed out. "They might be going the same way we are. Can you do that swerving through traffic thing to see if we can throw them?"

"You've seen too many movies." Matt waved a hand toward the window. "This is Melbourne traffic. You can't just swerve around without hitting anything. The moment we get to the lights, they'll be right behind us."

"They're not going to risk a magical battle in the middle of morning traffic." I wasn't so sure about that.

"They might assume the same thing about us," Matt said softly.

The blood drained out of my face. He was right. They may think we'd come quietly, so no one else got hurt. The assumption was a reasonable one. We were the good guys, after all.

"We need to stay ahead of them," Dyson said. He closed the window beside him. "And head in a different direction. There's no point in leading them toward the academy."

I chewed my lip but nodded. I wished Nash was here. Between us we had a dog, an owl, a gargoyle, and my gargoyle tattoo, with which I could conjure a magical creature to fight with me or for me. A dragon would turn the odds in our favour, even if it meant asking him to kill again.

"Right." Kane changed lanes and flew around a corner just before the lights turned red.

That move would have lost anyone law abiding, but the blue car swung around behind us. They ultimately worked for the government; they probably thought they were *above* the law.

A truck coming the other way beeped its horn and narrowly missed hitting the blue car. Shame, that would have slowed them down.

"Shit." Kane swerved to avoid a delivery van parked at the side of the road. He pulled back into our lane before another truck took out the side of our car. The driver stuck his finger out the window at us. I kept my hands on my lap to avoid doing the same thing back.

"We need to get out of the city," Matt urged.

"Have I mentioned this is my first time in Melbourne?" Kane asked. "I don't know where we're going unless it's programmed into the GPS."

"Turn left at the end of this street," Matt said. "We'll go west."

"Isn't that the direction we were going?" Dyson asked.

"Yeah, but we can get on a different road and head toward Ballarat. At least out in the country we can fight back without risk to too many others."

"If they realise that, they'll—" I stopped when another blue car rounded the turn in front of us and skidded to a stop. "Try to keep us from doing that," I finished.

"Hold on!" Kane spun the wheel and jammed his foot down on the accelerator. The car leapt forward and flew toward the second car. At the last moment he wrenched the steering wheel, but it wasn't enough. The side of his car scraped down the side of the blue one. The squeal of metal on metal made me wince and throw my hands over my ears.

"Dude!" Dyson shouted.

"Sorry!" Kane gunned the engine and we flew clear, but right into the path of another car.

We struck with a crunch of metal and glass. The airbags in front of Kane and Dyson inflated.

Apparently the car was too old to have any in the back. I was thrown forward hard. My seatbelt jerked and I came to a painful stop against the strap.

"Everyone out," Matt ordered. "Split up. Witch to shifter, shifter to hybrid."

Dyson groaned and rubbed his head, but he had his door open before I did.

He helped me out and grabbed my hand to pull me away from the car.

I glanced back once. "Fuck, there goes another suitcase full of clothes," I muttered.

Dyson snorted. "If that's the worst that happens…"

"Yeah, I know. We should stop talking now, I'm

making a bubble." I drew magic from a few small trees beside the road and made us both invisible. Our pursuers could hear us if we made a sound, but they wouldn't see us.

I turned my face just as Matt and Kane disappeared behind a bubble Matt made.

"Which way do we go?" Dyson whispered in my ear. Thank the gods magic allowed us to see each other and around ourselves.

"Anywhere but here," I said, "as long as we do it quietly."

Around us, Zeta agents, dressed from head to toe in black, climbed out of their cars, guns in hand. They stopped to listen, then moved in the direction they had seen us last.

I pulled Dyson in the opposite direction as fast as we dared to go.

"Give it up, witch," one of the agents called out.

Yeah, for real. As if that would make me surrender, just like that. It wasn't even worth a try. No witch I knew was that dumb. I certainly wasn't.

"Maybe I should let my gargoyle loose," I whispered.

"Can you do that and hold the bubble?" Dyson asked.

"I have no idea." I wasn't going to drop the bubble to find out.

One of the Zeta agents turned in our direction and pointed.

I froze. The only way they'd know where we were was if they had incredible hearing, like that of a dog.

The hybrids Zeta created were all what we would consider mythical creatures—phoenixes, griffins, gargoyles and, yes, dragons. What the hells kind of hybrid would a dog be?

"Have you ever heard of a Cerberus shifter?" I asked nervously.

"No, but that doesn't mean they don't exist," Dyson replied. "If you drop the bubble for long enough, I can distract him."

"I can't let you take that risk." I pulled him forward a few more steps.

The agent turned his face as though following our movement. His brow was creased. He moved toward us, slow and deliberate.

I stopped again.

The agent sniffed the air. He might be able to follow our scent as easily as any sound we may make. I could drop the bubble and blast him with magic, but that would draw the attention of every other Zeta agent on the street, not to mention the normal people who had stopped to gawk. Evidently a car crash was a novelty.

"We need some kind of distraction," Dyson whispered. "I can—"

Whatever he was about to say was interrupted by the flapping of wings. Not big wings, so it wasn't a dragon come to rescue us. No, these were small wings, but fast. An owl, about the size of my forearm, shot across the road and into the face of the Zeta agent.

The agent flailed his arms and tried to strike the bird, but Kane was gone as quickly as he'd arrived. He circled above the Zeta agent and came in for another dive.

"Shoot the fucker!" someone shouted.

Dyson squeezed my hand and dragged me up the street at a run.

A gunshot rang out.

I spun in time to see Kane soar away to the safety of a rooftop before he disappeared.

"Gods, Kane," Dyson muttered,

"You can thank him later." In the meantime, we had to keep running.

"We need to split up," Dyson insisted. "I'll throw that fucker off your scent."

Before I could protest, he let go of my hand and pushed his way out of the bubble.

"What the hells..." I almost lost my magic, but drew it back at the last moment. I hated the idea they would risk themselves because of me, but I wouldn't throw it back in their faces by exposing myself.

Dyson shifted into his dog form and let out a long, low howl.

"Over there!" an agent shouted. Three or four of them set off after him, including the dog hybrid.

"Peyton!" Matt's voice out of nowhere made me jump. Surrounded by his own bubble, I couldn't see him either. "Head west. I'll be right behind you."

"How do you know? You can't see me," I pointed out.

I was certain he grinned before he said, "I'll probably hear you trip over your own feet."

"I am not that clumsy," I retorted. Maybe he was the one tripping. In spite of that, I checked where the sun was and went in the opposite direction. A shadow passed overhead and I was relieved to see Kane land on a tree up ahead. I assumed Matt had told him which way we'd go. It seemed unfair I could see him and not vice versa, but there wasn't much I could do about that at the moment.

With one eye on him and the other on the side-walk ahead, I ducked around passers by and hurried away from the scene of the accident.

A big, furry figure bolted between a few cars in front of us. A couple of Zeta agents followed, but the gods knew where the rest were. I glanced back. The man I assumed was a dog hybrid was only fifty metres behind me and closing fast.

"Shit," I muttered.

"Take the next street," Matt said. "It'll be busy enough. Maybe we can throw him off."

"And if we can't?" I hissed.

"Then he'll meet with a nasty accident," Matt replied. He almost sounded as if he relished the idea.

"Right," I said under my breath. I hurried forward at a jog until I reached Clarendon Street. There, the roaring traffic would cover a lot of the noise and the exhaust fumes were thick. Hopefully thick enough to cover my scent.

I checked the sun and headed west toward the freeway. I hoped Matt had a plan. Dodging traffic doesn't generally result in a good life expectancy.

From the corner of my eye, I saw Kane on a roof up ahead. He looked around, obviously wondering where Matt and I were. Even in the middle of this craziness, I had to admit he was a cute owl. All brown and fluffy, I would have loved to give him a cuddle. Who am I kidding, I quite enjoyed cuddling his human form as well.

Something bumped into the back of me. I was about to curse when I realised it was Matt.

"I'd say you should watch where you're going, but…" I shrugged, then reminded myself he couldn't see that either.

He snorted. "We need to ditch this guy."

Sure enough, Cerberus was still following us.

"He's persistent," I agreed.

"Yeah. Hold on."

"To what?" I frowned. Matt grabbed my hand and pulled me toward him. At the same time, he expanded his bubble to incorporate us both. I let my magic go with a sigh of relief. Holding onto it for long periods of time was exhausting.

"I figured it would be easier if we could see each other," he said.

"I guess so," I agreed. He was still fully dressed, so he hadn't shifted into his gargoyle form during any of this. That was probably just as well, naked Matt would be distracting.

"I know you're there," Cerberus called out. "There is no escape. Give yourselves up now."

I rolled my eyes and mouthed, "No way, motherfucker."

Matt grinned. "Let's try something," he mouthed back.

He gripped my hand and we bolted into the traffic.

3

THE CARS COULDN'T SEE us, so none of the drivers were any wiser about how close they came to hitting us. A side mirror grazed my ass and I bit back a yelp. Later, they might wonder why it sat at a different angle. For now though, the driver drove on, seemingly oblivious.

Matt tugged me across the last lane in front of a huge truck. We managed to leap onto the sidewalk with a hair's width to spare.

"Now I know you're crazy, as well as an asshole," I said lightly. I rubbed my backside. That would bruise later.

"We made it, didn't we?" He loosened his grip on my hand and jerked his head back. "Him, on the other hand—"

Cerberus stood on the opposite side of the road, a scowl on his features. He sniffed the air. His scowl deepened. I assumed he could still smell us, but the fumes from the cars confounded his doggie senses.

"Come on," Matt tugged me away from Cerberus and toward the highway. "We need a car."

"You're not suggesting we steal one, are you?" I frowned at him.

He ignored the question. "Do you have your phone?"

"Of course." I patted the back pocket of my shorts. "Do you want me to try to conjure a car?"

He gave me a funny look. "No, can you order a ride share car?"

"Oh." Now I felt silly. "Only if you have cash. Zeta would trace any cards we use."

He gave me a look as if I'd said the sky was blue. "I've got us covered for that."

I shrugged with my spare shoulder and tapped the details for the ride share into the app with my thumb. The moment I pressed, "enter" my breath caught in my throat.

"What if they're tracing my phone?" I asked.

"Then our friend over there would know where we are. But just in case—" Matt grabbed the device from my hand and tossed it onto the road. It was promptly run over and crushed by a pizza truck.

Yes, a pizza truck. I have never felt so betrayed by my favourite food in my entire life.

"What the fuck?" I asked.

"Would you rather be in a Zeta lab? I can leave you to it, if you'd prefer." He made to step away.

"Don't you dare," I hissed. I gritted my teeth and shook my head. "It's just a phone."

"Exactly." He nodded. "Now hurry up or we'll miss the ride share car altogether."

We trotted down the block and around a corner. Finally out of sight of the Zeta agents, Matt dropped the bubble and my hand.

"We can't leave without Dyson and Kane." I looked around, but saw no sign of either of them, dog, owl or naked men.

"We can and we will," Matt insisted. "They can both take care of themselves. My job is to get you to the academy in one piece."

I swallowed. On one hand, he was right. We couldn't afford to take the risk of waiting for them to find us. On the other hand, I adored them both and if anything happened to them because of me…

I gave my head a little shake. If they were injured, or worse, it would be because of Zeta, not me. The fact they found it necessary to protect me was Zeta's fault. However, I would blame myself until the end of time.

I sucked in a breath. "We can wait until the car arrives." If I still had my phone, I would know how long that was. Since I didn't, I crossed my arms over my chest and kept my eyes open for the guys.

Matt placed a hand on my shoulder. "They'll be fine. They're both tough as nails and slightly more intelligent."

I snorted. "I thought you guys were friends?"

"We are, but I was trying to make you smile." He shrugged indifferently.

"Why bother?" I asked. "We loathe each other, remember?"

He grinned. "Yes, we do. That doesn't mean we can't be nice, though."

"I suppose." I scanned the rooftops. Gods, please don't let them catch the guys. A bird took off and my heart leapt until I realised it was just a pigeon.

A moment later, a car drew up alongside us. A man with spiky blue hair and about a bajillion facial piercings stuck his head out the window and smiled.

"Hey, you ordered a Broomer?"

"Yeah, we did," I opened the door to the back seat, while Matt sat beside the driver.

"Where to, guys?" the driver asked cheerfully.

Matt gave him the address while I fastened my seatbelt and watched out the window.

"Wacca's restaurant, Werribee," the driver repeated. "Okay, great! That'll take us about half an hour in this traffic." He pulled his little yellow car away from the curb.

Mat nodded. "Okay, Broomer."

"Call me Bruce," the driver said. "It's my name, but don't wear it out." He laughed, which would have been infectious under other circumstances.

"Hilarious," I muttered.

"Yeah, my friends agree. They tell me I should stop talking so much, but what can I say? I'm a friendly guy."

I hunkered down in my seat and kept my eyes on the city as it passed by. Bruce kept up a monologue the entire time, while Matt responded with a word or two here and there. I didn't hear a thing they said until Bruce pulled his car into a parking space at Wacca's.

Matt handed over a couple of notes and we climbed out of the car.

"Have a great day!" Bruce waved out the window as he drove off.

"I think he might be more annoying than you are," Matt remarked.

"Is that even possible?" I asked ironically.

Matt looked thoughtful. "You're right, it probably isn't. You set the bar pretty high."

"If I had a bar right now, I'd shove it up your ass," I murmured.

He chuckled. "We have quite a walk in front of us. Let's get something to eat first. My shout."

"It will have to be, since I have no money and no phone." I gave him a look.

"You're welcome," he said lightly. "This isn't quite how I expected our first date to go."

I gave him a funny look. "You expected us to have a first date?"

"No. That's exactly my point." He opened the door.

I stuck my tongue out at him and marched past.

"Always with the class," he said reproachfully.

"Maybe a Zeta lab wouldn't be so bad." I sat at a more-or-less clean table near a window so I could watch while we ate.

Matt's eyes flashed with anger. "Trust me, it wouldn't," he said in a tight voice before he stalked away.

While I regretted my words, I glanced at the few

people around the small restaurant. None looked in my direction. They were either lost in conversation or, more commonly, engrossed in their phones. I couldn't see what they were looking at, but I wasn't sure they'd notice if Kane and Dyson walked through the door, naked.

Matt slammed a tray down in front of me, making me jump.

"I'm sorry about what I said. I didn't mean to—"

"Yeah, whatever." He slipped into the seat opposite me. "I get it. You ran your mouth off about something you know nothing about."

"And you do?" I asked as gently as I could.

"I'm not talking about that with you, especially not here," he snapped. He pushed a box of food and a cup of tea toward me and started to eat.

I sighed and opened my box. Bacon, eggs, toast—all the essentials for an early lunch.

"Eat fast, we shouldn't linger around here for too long."

I was too anxious to be hungry, and still full from breakfast, but I managed to down everything in record time. I picked up my tea to wash it down when Matt rose.

"Bring it with you. You can sip and walk."

I grabbed up my cup, put my rubbish in the bin

and followed him out. "How did you know I drank tea?"

He shrugged. "Lucky guess."

I gave him a disbelieving look. "Bullshit. If you were guessing, you would have given me coffee. Or water."

"You must have mentioned it in passing then." He led us back to the road and we started off to the south.

"Well, thanks," I said awkwardly. "It saved me from having to tell you coffee is disgusting."

He gave me a sideways glance and sipped his. "I knew there was something wrong with you."

"Fuck off," I retorted. "There's probably a lot of things wrong with me. Not drinking coffee isn't one."

"Oh yeah? What are the others?"

I sniffed. "I'm not going to dignify that question with a response."

"Coward."

I glanced toward him to see his eyes shining and a smile tugging at the corners of his mouth.

"Has anyone told you you're an asshole?" I asked.

"Yes, you have. Recently, too."

I smiled sweetly. "Has it sunk in yet?"

He grinned. "Honey, it sank in a long time ago."

I blushed. "You wish."

He let out a choking laugh. "Not a chance."

"Liar."

He shrugged. "Keep telling yourself that. In the meantime, can you walk a little faster?"

"Can you shift and I'll ride on your back?" I was only half-joking.

Rather than dismiss the suggestion offhand, he looked thoughtful. "I don't think it's come to that yet. We'll call that plan B."

"Fine. As long as we don't get to plan F."

"The day I go to plan F with you…" he started.

"Yes?" I prompted.

He gave me a look which suggested only the animosity between us was stopping him from dragging me into the bushes and screwing me silly.

He shook his head. "I'll know I've lost the last of my common sense."

"You said 'willpower' wrong." I stepped over a fallen log.

"Lucky I have plenty of that," he shot back.

"Oh really?" Without thinking, I turned and pressed my palm to his cheek. I don't know who moved next, but our lips were pressed together, and his tongue slipped inside my mouth.

I only kissed him back for the count of three.

Okay, four. All right, maybe it was thirty seconds, tops. I pulled back and smiled. "Yep, you're totally willpower man."

He scowled at me as though I had done something horribly wrong and stalked on ahead.

"Hurry up, we're nearly here," he growled.

I shrugged to myself and followed. "There's nothing wrong with being attracted to someone."

"It is when they're a pain in your ass," he said over his shoulder.

"I'm not that bad when you get to know me," I said. "I—"

"Shhh," he hissed.

I immediately froze. Every centimetre of me watched and listened for…anything. "What is it?" I said finally.

"The University of Arcana."

"Is it under attack?" Please gods, don't let it be that, after all we've been through already.

"No, I'm just not sure I should take you there," he replied.

I frowned and stepped up closer to him. "Why not? What's wrong?" A heavy feeling started to settle in my stomach. Had he sensed some kind of danger I couldn't? Did he have heightened gargoyle senses, like Cerberus seemed to have dog instincts?

"If I take you there," he said slowly, "I'll be stuck with you around for the entire academic year."

I punched him on the arm as hard as I could.

While he grinned, I stomped past him and onto the university slash academy grounds.

At last.

4

THE UNIVERSITY WAS HOUSED in a mansion which was over a hundred years old. A number of signs dotted the driveway which led to it. One read, "Danger." Another said, "Condemned." Fortunately trees and hedges obscured the view from the road or people would notice it was neither of those things. At least, the building *looked* safe enough.

The inhabitants, on the other hand, were probably a different story.

A group of students strolled past and didn't give us more than a glance. At least, I assumed they were students. They were all dressed in blue jackets, blue and white ties and blue trousers or skirts.

"For real? UA has a uniform?" I snorted.

"Yeah, and we have to wear it, too," Matt replied.

My smile faded. "You're kidding?"

He shrugged with one shoulder. "Not this time. At least the skirts aren't plaid."

I made a face. "Thank the gods for small mercies." At this point I was distracting myself from worrying about Dyson and Kane. "We need to tell them about Zeta coming after us again."

Matt nodded. "Let me deal with that. You go and get settled."

"What about you?" I asked.

Before I got an answer, he was gone, marching toward what I assumed was the admin section of the campus. As for me, I was engulfed in a hug.

"Peyton, you got here finally!"

"Ariana." I gave her a squeeze, then leaned back to look her in the face. "You got here, too."

She smiled. "Last night. Where are the others? I saw Matt's back as I stepped out of our dorm." She wrinkled her nose. "If you can call it that. They've brought in temporary buildings for those of us who decided to stay with the AMM."

"Are there so few of us?" I fell into step beside her.

She led me toward a series of low buildings set off to one side from the mansion.

"Of the original six hundred or so, there's only

about three hundred coming." She opened the door and stepped into a long, narrow corridor. "Just under thirty students died in the attack last spring. I guess the rest didn't feel safe here."

"Or they know Melbourne winters suck," I said dryly.

"That too," she agreed. "Where is all your stuff?"

I told her about the attack on us and explained about the guys. "I'm sure they'll turn up sooner or later." I sighed.

She gave me another hug. "I'm sure they will. They're tough, smart guys."

"Yes, they are." I remembered what Matt said and flipped him a mental bird. What did he know anyway?

"So, this is our room." Ariana pulled out a regular key and unlocked it.

I stepped inside and gaped in dismay. The room was tiny. So small it only contained two small cupboards, side by side and a bunk bed. I doubted a heater would do much for the chill in the air.

"I took the top bunk. I hope you don't mind?" She looked tentative, but I didn't think it had anything to do with which bed she'd chosen. We'd left the previous year on uneasy terms and had only seen each other via video chat since.

"I don't mind," I said. "Your snoring might be muffled by the ceiling, with any luck."

She giggled. "And yours might be muffled by the underside of my bed."

"Not a chance," I said lightly. "I'm guessing there isn't a bathroom connected to this room?"

Ariana grimaced. "It's not even in this building. Everyone has to shower in the next one over. Meanwhile, the UA students live in a nice warm mansion." She wrinkled her nose.

"Oh good, elitism," I said sarcastically. "Maybe I should tell them who my mother is. They might take pity on us and give us better accommodation."

"You can try," she said wryly. "But I have a feeling they won't care."

I exhaled through my nose. "Do we really have to wear that uniform?"

"So I'm told." She looked just as happy about that as I felt. "At least you'll look cute in it."

I barked a laugh. "Is it too late to transfer to Melbourne Uni?" They, like everywhere but here, had no uniforms for students. Shame they didn't teach magic.

"Probably," she replied, "there are other options, like getting a job arranging flowers."

I looked at her in surprise. "Why flowers?"

She shrugged. "Why not? It might be fun."

"I suppose so." I ran a hand over my face. "I should go and check in with the academy admin and see about a new phone and a uniform. Have you seen Nash?" My blood heated at the idea of seeing him again, being alone with him, his hands on my…

Ariana cleared her throat and brought me back to reality. "Not yet. I've only seen Hamish and a few others." Her face went slightly pink.

"Hamish? Really?" The last I heard, he was interested in her, but she didn't feel the same. Apparently things had changed.

"We came here together," she explained. "We might have bonded on the drive down. He's sweet."

I smiled. "I'm thrilled for you." He was nice and she deserved to be happy. "Just let him know if he hurts you, I'll conjure a gargoyle to tear his nuts off."

Ariana giggled. "Come on, I'll show you where the academy admin is. They're a little hard to find."

"Don't tell me, they've been shoved down into the university basement?" I said, half joking.

She gave me a funny look. "How did you know?"

"Lucky guess." I had a feeling the academy was the university's poor cousin and would be treated accordingly until we got a new, more permanent campus. Hopefully that wouldn't take long. I hated wearing uniforms, especially ones that screamed, "repressed private school girl." I was too old for that.

Before Ariana led me out the door, she handed me a key. "Apparently we have to learn to do a few things the old-fashioned way."

I pocketed the key and grimaced. "Welcome to the nineteen hundreds. Population: us."

"Basement" was an understatement. The space allocated for the academy admin was dark, dank, and smelled as if they kept rats locked inside for a few decades. Two tiny windows at the top of the wall would allow for an emergency escape, but didn't let in much light. A handful of bulbs hung from the ceiling, but several flickered. Instant headache stuff right there.

The man behind the desk looked weary. They had probably spent the holidays trying to pull enough resources together to get the academy ready in time. Their surroundings wouldn't have inspired them much.

"Can I help you?" he asked.

I explained the situation. As I talked, he seemed more and more interested.

"Zeta came after you, you say?" He clicked his tongue. "Terrible business, that." He reached into a drawer and pulled out a new phone, still in its box. "Try not to let this one get damaged. We should have a uniform in your size. The university has been very generous with *those*."

I didn't miss the inflection. Nor did Ariana, judging by the look on her face.

I grimaced. "It is a bit cozy in here."

He snorted. "It's only temporary."

"Fingers crossed," Ariana said lightly. "Can Peyton try on some clothes?"

"Sure." He waved us toward what looked like a storeroom. "Take whatever you need." He rubbed his chin. "Are you all right for a ride into town to replace your other clothes?"

"I should be fine, yes," I said. I wanted to ask for someone to drive me around to look for the guys. Instead, I just said, "Thank you."

He gave a nod and turned back to his work.

THE LIGHT in the storeroom was as bad as the rest of the space, but it was enough to see shelves with bags of shirts, pants, skirts, and ties. Jackets hung from a rack to one side.

"At least it's better than being chased by Zeta," I remarked. "Although they might laugh if they saw me in this stuff." I shut the door and pulled out a few bags marked with my size. "Surely there are pants for women in here somewhere."

"If you find any, let me know." Ariana reclined against the door. "I feel silly in this skirt."

I glanced toward her. "You look cute. I'm sure Hamish would agree." I gave her a sly smile.

She flushed and muttered, "He said he did."

I grinned and pulled on a stiff university shirt and skirt. The skirt fell to just above my knees. I frowned at it for a moment.

"I guess it's not too bad. It *could* be ankle length." The shirt hugged my breasts in a way I actually liked. Maybe naughty schoolgirl wasn't such a bad look after all.

"That would be very impractical when running away from bad guys," Ariana said. "For the record, it makes your legs and ass look amazing."

"Thanks." I wondered what the guys would think. To be fair, they would all be dressed more or less the same, except Nash. Unless this place had a dress code for teachers, too. Maybe they'd make him wear a suit. My mouth went dry at the idea and I actually licked my lips.

"This should be your size." Ariana handed me a jacket. "The good news is, I've seen plenty of students without their jackets on. I think they're only for when it's cold."

I took the jacket and shrugged it on. "I miss my oversized *Harry Potter* sweater already." It was old and worn, but comfortable. The jacket was stiff and cold, but better than nothing.

"I hear you," she sighed. "I miss my pink hoodie. It was my favourite thing to wear, by far."

I remembered a pale pink hoodie with paint stains and holes. I'm not sure I would miss seeing her in it, but comfort was a good thing.

"Okay, I think I'm done." I grabbed two more shirts and another skirt before we stepped out of the storeroom. "No sign of the guys yet, I suppose." If they turned up, they weren't here, looking for clothes to wear. The idea of the twins naked made my heart race again.

"They'll turn up," Ariana said. "I promise."

"I hope so," I replied. "Otherwise, I might have to go out and look for them."

"I'll come with you," Ariana assured me. "If it

comes to that. We'll stick together and look after each other."

"You mean you'll keep an eye on me," I said, more tersely than I'd intended.

She blanched and her tongue darted over her lips. "I said I was sorry—" she started.

I put a hand on her shoulder and squeezed lightly. "No, *I'm* sorry. I don't want you to think I'm holding a grudge. I'm really not. You were trying to look out for me and I adore you for it. I didn't mean to be a bitch, it's just been a difficult day already." That was a lame excuse. I needed to try to be a better friend.

She leaned over to put her arms around me. "I adore you, too. I'm sorry they came after you. I should have been there. My unicorn could have stabbed them with her horn." She raised her arm. Her sleeve was rolled back to show the tattoo of a unicorn with a multicoloured mane Matt inked on her last year.

"Thank you, but too many humans would have seen it. We don't want to have it broadcast on the evening news." I could just imagine it. *Unicorn spotted in peak-hour traffic, authorities baffled.*

She grinned. "I suppose not, but she's ready if we go looking for the guys."

I chuckled. "So is my gargoyle. Let's wait a few more hours, then if they're not here, we'll go and hunt them down. I'm sure Kane and Dyson can't be too far away."

"Absolutely not," a new voice said. "You're *not* going back out there to look for them."

I turned to see Nash. Holy fucking instant orgasms, he looked good in a suit. Better than good. I wanted to tear it straight off him and…

I cleared my throat. "I beg your pardon, sir?"

His pupils dilated at that, and a bulge formed at the front of his pants. He liked it when I called him sir.

"Ariana, will you excuse us please?" Nash said, his voice tight. "I need to talk to Peyton alone."

"Yes, sir," she squeaked and hurried away.

Nash took my arm. "Come with me," he said softly.

Fuck yeah, I thought you'd never ask.

5

Nash led me to a room on the ground floor of the main university building. His body was tense the entire walk there, eyes darting back and forth.

"Are you expecting another Zeta attack?" I asked after the third time he stopped to look around.

"No." He pulled me into a room and closed the door. "Things are different here. The academy might have frowned on us associating, if they had known, but the UA strictly forbids it, under threat of being fired."

I raised both eyebrows at him in surprise.

Before I could speak, he held up a hand. "I know. We're two adults conducting a consensual relationship." He stalked to the window and drew the curtains closed over it.

"Does that mean we can't see each other anymore?" My heart sank. I was falling for him hard, and I was falling for Kane and Dyson. Nash would still be my teacher, so I would see him whenever we did self-defence training, or practice for the hand-to-hand combat team. None of that would be the same.

He turned back and licked his lips. "I thought it might be a good idea if we stopped for a while, but seeing you in that outfit makes me want to tear it off and screw you silly." He stalked toward me. His eyes blazed with desire.

I couldn't imagine even trying to resist him when he looked like that. My whole body ached. I needed him inside me, buried deep. I needed him to touch me.

I sucked in a deep breath. "Oh, really?" I toyed with the top button of my shirt. The back of my wrist brushed past my hard nipple. "Naughty school-girl does it for you, hmmm?"

He snorted. "*You* do it for me. I don't care what you're wearing. Although, the uniform does add a certain something."

I cocked my head to one side. "Yeah. That suit is pretty hot, too, sir."

He glanced down and grimaced. "I feel ridiculous. I teach self-defence, I'm not a lawyer."

"Flashbacks to your police days?" I asked. I regretted the words the moment I said them. In his past life, he had had to kill to defend himself and people he cared about. At the academy, he had done it again, in his dragon form. Reminding him of those dark days wasn't fair to him.

A frown crossed his face, but it was quickly gone, replaced by pure desire. "I don't want to think about that now." He grabbed my hand and pulled me to him. His deft hands made quick work of my buttons. He slipped my shirt down my arms and carefully placed it over the back of a chair. He hated mess.

He claimed my mouth with his. His tongue probed deeply while he reached around to unhook my bra.

I let it slide off my arms and pressed my bare nipples to the front of his suit jacket. One of my hands wandered down to the front of his pants. He was already rock hard. I undid the front and slipped my hand inside. My fingers curled around his hot erection.

He groaned and broke off our kiss just long enough to shed his jacket and shirt, then took my wrists in one hand and turned me around. He pushed me toward a table and bent me over the top. With one hand, he pinned me to the wood while with the other, he slid his hand up my skirt and tugged my panties down.

I kicked them aside just as he positioned himself and slid his cock into me. I let out a moan of pure pleasure.

"I've missed you," I said, breathless already.

"I missed you too." He clamped a hand on my hip and drove himself deeper inside me.

The thrill of doing something truly elicit sent a thrill down my spine and all across my body. Without meaning to, I came. Pleasure wracked my whole body and I cried out. I bit my lip to keep from making too much noise. That would give us away for sure.

"It seems you missed me a lot," he said, uncharacteristically teasing.

I laughed softly, but it quickly turned into a groan as he began to thrust more rhythmically. I leaned down to rest my cheek on the cool wood. At this angle he was filling me fully. With each stroke, his balls slapped against me.

"Gods," he whispered. He pulled out and let my wrists go. His hands slid down my body as he lowered himself to his knees. His tongue flicked at my folds.

I reached out to grip the sides of the table as his tongue delved deeper. He rubbed the tip hard against my clit. I wanted to rock against him, but between his mouth and the table, I was pinned, helpless to do anything but let my passion rise again.

"Sir, I'm going to come again," I said in a rough whisper.

"No you're not." He pulled away just before I wcnt over the edge.

I groaned in frustration.

He chuckled. "Not yet." He peeled me off the table and helped me out of my skirt. "You look better out of that uniform."

"You look better out of that suit, sir."

He was slender, but fit. His arms and legs were defined by muscle. A light sprinkle of hair dusted his chest and abs and ended in curls at the base of his stomach.

I looked at him sideways. "That is particularly adorable, sir." I pointed to his feet. He was completely naked except for a pair of superhero socks.

He grinned and leaned on the table to tug them

off. "I had other things on my mind," he said unapologetically.

He took my hand and led me to his bed. He sat me down on the side and knelt in front of me to bury his face between my legs. His lips and tongue masterfully lapped against my clit and between my folds. He slid two fingers into my wetness, then three, and started to stroke me inside and out.

I gathered up small sections of blanket in my hands and gripped tight while he drove me to another orgasm. This time, he let me come so hard I had to grit my teeth to keep from screaming.

I hadn't even come down fully when he drew me the rest of the way onto the bed.

"Get on your hands and knees," he said, his voice deeper with lust.

"Yes, sir." I did as he asked before he settled himself behind me and slid into me up the hilt. He reached around to cup my breasts with both hands.

"I don't care what they say," he growled between thrusts. "I'm not going to give you up. I'd rather lose my job."

"We'll be careful." The way his palms rubbed my nipples made it hard to think, much less talk. "You won't have to give up anything."

His strokes came faster and faster. "Gods, Peyton, you feel so good."

"So do you, sir," I replied.

He let out a long, low grunt and with a few more frantic thrusts, he came inside me. The heat of his cock and his cum made me come for a third time.

We both flopped down and panted for a while, his hands still on my breasts, cock deep inside me.

"I could stay like this forever," he said with a sigh.

"I don't know about forever, but we have a while." I lay with my back to him, one leg over his to hold him inside. There was something incredibly intimate about lying there full like this.

He lightly caressed my breasts and traced circles around and over my nipples.

"Sometimes I wish we could run away and find a place where we could lie in bed naked all day." He sounded wistful. "Of course if we do, you'll want to bring the others."

"Right." That brought me back to Dyson and Kane, but they fled my mind when Nash started to move inside me again.

"I wouldn't object, as long as you're happy." He thrust a little faster. "And make some time for me." And faster.

"And call you 'sir'?" I asked.

His thumbs and fingers tightened on my nipples, painful but pleasant.

"And that." His strokes became quicker and firmer.

His hold on my nipples became a pinch which filled me with ecstasy I had never felt before.

"Mmmm, harder, sir, please."

He grunted and obliged by ramming into me so hard it hurt.

"Again," I pleaded. "Harder."

He did it again and again until I was caught between begging him to stop and coming harder than I ever had. In the end I cried out as I was swamped by a fourth orgasm, then a fifth. Both swept me away until I could no longer think. Every nerve, every muscle was given over to absolute pleasure.

Somewhere in the back of my awareness, I heard and felt him come again. He cried out my name and then all the pain was gone, replaced by lethargy in every last little bit of me.

I lay like a rag doll, my eyes half open, panting for a long while.

"Oh my gods," I breathed. "That was…"

"Yes," he agreed, "it was. You're incredible."

"No, you, sir," I replied sleepily.

He slid out of me. I would hurt like hells later, but I had no regrets.

"Are you arguing with me?" he asked.

"Would I dare?" I rolled over to face him.

He regarded me for a moment. "Yes. Yes you would. Lucky I'm here to keep you in line. Otherwise you'd tear off and do gods only know what."

That brought Dyson and Kane right back to my mind with a jolt which made me fully awake.

I sat up. "We need to go looking for the guys."

"No, you need to stay here where it's safe," he said firmly. The crease between his brows deepened. I probably imagined the slight glow of his eyes and the hint of scales on his cheeks.

"Is that what this was about? Distracting me from them?"

He blinked. "I needed you. Wanted you. You wanted me, too." He averted his eyes.

He was right, my brain had been firmly in my clitoris.

I sagged. "If anything happens to them…"

Nash put his arms around me and drew me close. "If anyone can take of themselves, it's those two." He placed a finger under my chin and made me look at him. "They're resilient. They will be fine, okay? And if they don't turn up by morning, I'll go out there myself."

"Are you going to go all dragon on them?" I asked, half teasing.

He hesitated. For a moment, I thought he might be angry, but then he smiled. "Would it turn you on if I did?"

"Yes," I replied firmly. "But only after I've replenished my energy." I covered a yawn with my hand. "You've worn me out, sir."

He chuckled softly. "I have? I haven't even begun yet." He rolled me onto my back and moved down my body to suck my nipple.

"Maybe one more time," I said breathlessly. Gods, the man would drive me crazy and I would enjoy every moment of it.

6

MIDNIGHT CAME and went before I finally crawled into bed. Thank the gods I had the bottom bunk. I doubt I would have made it to the top one.

I fell asleep to the sound of Ariana snoring and woke as the sun slanted in through the window.

I shot up and hit my head on the bunk above me.

"Shit." I rubbed my head and leaned against the wall.

"Are you all right down there?" Ariana's face appeared, upside down.

"Yeah, all good. I'll just have to remember to sit up more slowly from now on." I rose carefully and grabbed a change of clothes.

I had showered—yes, with Nash—the night before, so I just dressed and brushed my hair. I caught a glimpse of myself in the mirror and grimaced.

I still had the streak of green hair. I had gotten used to it. Mostly. Truthfully though, I looked tired. Satisfied, but tired. My body ached in the best way possible. Even so, I would have killed for a long soak in a hot bath.

I had to step to one side to let Ariana climb down and dress. We were both all but pressed against the walls in an effort to keep out of each other's way.

"This is a little too cozy," I said after ducking her elbow for the third time. "At least they've given the teachers more space." I told her about Nash's room and how we'd have to keep our liaisons secret.

"That's exciting," she grinned, her eyes wide. "The thrill of the forbidden."

I sighed. "I suppose so, but it's a bit silly to make consenting adults hide. I mean, who are we hurting?"

She paused for a moment. "You could be hurt if he fails you."

"He would never do that," I replied quickly. After a moment I added, "And I wouldn't give him an excuse to."

"I know you wouldn't on purpose, but you could pass without going to his classes if you wanted."

I was about to argue, but realised she was right. I

did have an unfair advantage over the other students. "I'll make sure that doesn't happen," I said firmly.

"I know you will." She gave me a hug and opened the door. "Ready to face the dining room?"

"Why does that sound as if I'm going to my execution?" I grabbed my jacket and followed her out the door.

"Because you haven't really met any of the UA students yet," she replied. She wrinkled her nose. "It's like we smell of AMM or something."

"What does AMM smell like?" I hung my jacket over my arm and followed her toward the main building.

"I don't know." She laughed, but it faded almost immediately. "Dyson might."

I sighed. "He's probably in the dining hall, eating all of the bacon."

"That's possible," she agreed. "We should hurry, before it's all gone."

I didn't think either of us thought that was true, but we walked faster anyway.

THE DINING HALL WAS HUGE; probably bigger than

the accommodation UA set aside for us. The chatter didn't skip a beat as we entered, but eyes turned to stare at us anyway. I saw what Ariana meant. They seemed to know we were from a different school, even though we all wore the same uniform.

I lifted my chin and walked toward the food service area. "I'm having flashbacks to high school," I muttered. "Bad ones."

"Same," Ariana replied. "They really don't want us here, do they?"

I met a few hostile glances with my own and they turned away.

"Too bad, they have to deal, just like we do," I said firmly.

There was no sign of either Dyson or bacon amongst the warming trays of food. Rather, every-thing looked… I groaned softly. Healthy.

"Are they trying to kill us?" Ariana asked. She grabbed herself a bowl of oats and fruit and made a face at the bottles of skim milk before she poured some onto her cereal. "There's not even coffee."

"Thank the gods there's tea," I said, until I realised it was all the herbal stuff. "You're right, they *are* trying to kill us." Or have us kill each other in a caffeine-withdrawal induced rage.

"It might do you some good." Matt appeared behind me, his usual guarded expression on his face.

"Not a chance," I replied. "But remember that when I'm ripping your head off because I need the carbs."

He chuckled. "I would have thought a fitness fanatic like you would enjoy this kind of food." He gestured toward the large variety of fruit.

"I like fitness," I agreed, "but I also like flavour." In spite of that, I snagged two bananas and a tub of yoghurt. A girl had to eat. Later I might ask Nash to smuggle me some chocolate. "Any word on the guys?"

"*Now* you ask," he said reproachfully. "No, there's been no word."

"I should be out there looking, too."

"That's a good idea," Matt nodded. "You should absolutely put others at risk again, just to satisfy your ego."

I rolled my eyes. "Fuck off. I just want to help. It's my fault they're missing."

"Your help won't find them sooner," he replied. He picked up an apple and bit into it.

"You don't know that." I picked up a spoon and resisted the urge to stab him in the eye with the blunt end.

"I know Zeta will be looking for you."

"As if I need reminding of that." I made a face.

"Then go to class and let people more qualified deal with Zeta. The guys will be fine without your help." The look on his face made me want to slap him. So much for our uneasy peace.

"I don't…"

I stopped talking as a UA student with a broad chest stepped between us.

"Don't mind me," he said, his voice a pleasant rumble. He picked up an orange and started to peel it. "I couldn't help but overhear. You're the one Zeta came after?" His ocean blue eyes held no hint of his opinion of either me or Zeta.

"They came after the whole academy," I snapped. I was in no mood for more accusations.

"But because of you, they knew where to look?" Still, his expression gave away nothing.

"It's not that simple." I frowned.

He smiled, just slightly. "Simple enough that your presence puts us all in danger. Apparently it's already done that, if the mention of missing guys is an indication." His brow quirked upward in question.

I flushed. "It's complicated."

"It's really very simple," he said slowly. "You

should leave before you get anyone else killed." With that, he turned and stalked away.

Tears prickled at the corners on my eyes. "Maybe he's right."

"Hey." Ariana put her cereal on the table beside her and put an arm around me. "He's *not* right. You deserve an education as much as he does. Maybe more. This place should be safe, right?" She looked toward Matt.

"It should be," he agreed. "It's been here for at least a hundred years, teaching paranormals and breeding bigots like that." He patted my arm. "Do what I said—go to class and forget all about this."

I swear, if he had said, "Don't trouble your pretty little head," I would have decked him then and there.

"I will go to class, but I'm not going to forget. Not until the guys are back here, safe and sound."

Matt shrugged and walked away. Damn, why did he have to be such an asshole with a perfect ass? I didn't know what I wanted to do more, cup it or kick it.

"Is it possible they decided not to come back?" Ariana asked as we searched for a place to sit. "Maybe they agree with that guy." She gestured to where Asshole 2.0 sat with a group of friends.

Every now and again they would all look in our

direction and glare. I fought down the urge to climb onto a table and scream at the top of my lungs, "This isn't fucking high school, you morons!"

Instead, I slid down in my chair and sliced banana into my yoghurt.

"If there's one thing I know about those two, it's that they'll be back." As long as they are able to. "They're both dedicated to their educations."

"And to you," Ariana said slyly. "I know they're both hoping you'll choose them some day."

I blushed. She was right. They made that clear enough. I told them I wouldn't choose either of them if I came between them, but they still vied for my attention.

"Right. If they don't come back, you-know-who would win by default." This place had far too many ears for me to say Nash's name out loud.

"I'm sure he wouldn't mind." She smiled.

"Hey." Hamish Small flopped down in the seat beside her and kissed her cheek.

While she flushed, I smiled. It was nice to see her happy and Hamish was a nice guy.

"Looks like AMM has its own table," he remarked.

That proved accurate when more and more of our fellow academy students filed into the hall and sat with us. Violette, Mustafa, and Carter I knew already. Some other faces looked familiar, some not. Everyone seemed as anxious as I felt.

"Do we have to take classes with them?" Violette moaned.

"I don't think so," Carter replied. They had changed their hair to solid black during the holidays. It was an interesting look. "They have their own lecturers."

"I heard Mr Nash will be working with them as well as us," Mustafa remarked.

I swung my head to look at him in surprise. "Who did you hear that from?" I asked.

He shrugged. "One of the UA girls. They were talking about how hot he was." Mustafa made a face, but he watched me carefully. A couple of dozen AMM students had seen him kiss me outside the bus before we were evacuated from the old campus.

I shrugged. "Student-teacher relations are forbidden here," I said as lightly as I could. "So all they're going to get to do is look."

Mustafa nodded, but he didn't look convinced.

I wasn't either, truthfully. The idea of Nash touching another woman made me want to claw her eyes out, but technically he owed me nothing. I was seeing two other guys, after all. When they weren't missing, that was. I told myself jealousy was stupid, but I didn't believe it.

"We'll mostly be relegated to our classrooms," Carter said. "At least until they find us somewhere else."

"Let's hope that's soon." Asshole 2.0 stopped at the table to regard us as if we were a nest of cockroaches. Did cockroaches even have nests? I didn't know, but that was what his expression looked like.

One of his friends laughed. "My father said they should just close the AMM and be done with it. It's nothing more than a second rate university to begin with."

"You're right, Jacob," Asshole 2.0 said. "Second rate at best. Maybe third."

"You know Xav, I think you might be right." Jacob sneered and moved on.

Xav—short for Xavier, I assumed—lingered for a while longer, hostile eyes on me.

I gave him an eye roll. "Are you done with your preschool crap? If so, then fuck off."

A flash of anger crossed his eyes. He stepped closer to me. "You'll leave here, if it's the last thing I do."

I stood and drew myself up to my impressive

height, which brought my face all the way up to his chin—he was tall, okay, be quiet—and glared.

"Don't make idle threats," I hissed.

He snorted. "It's not an idle threat, bitch. You're a danger to everyone here. You'll leave if I have to carry you out of here myself."

Before I could respond, or punch him, he turned and walked away.

Fucker.

7

THE PARANORMAL HISTORY classroom was freezing. I ran my hands up and down my arms to keep warm.

"I think I know what I want to do when I finish studying," I said.

"Heater installer?" Ariana said hopefully. Her lips were slightly blue and her hands trembled.

I laughed, but it was almost as bitter as the cold. "No, I think I want to teach."

"Like Dyson?" She gave me a meaningful look. "Are you choosing him?"

I frowned. "No. I mean, I'm not not choosing him, I just…" I shook my head. "I mean, teaching at a place like this."

"What, cold?"

I chuckled. "No, like a university. Maybe not one

where people are assholes to other paranormals, but..."

She nodded. "I get it. You want to work with Nash. Are you—" She stopped talking as my eyes widened in warning. "I was going to ask if you're inspired by him?"

I held back a snort. *Sure* she was. "Yes, very inspired. Who wouldn't want to teach young paranormals to defend themselves?"

"Can you teach me?" she asked. "I think Mr Nash has pretty much given up on me."

It was not in his nature to give up, but I was happy to give her extra help. "Of course, I—"

"Shhh," Violette hissed, "I'm trying to listen."

"Sorry," I mouthed. I rubbed my hands up and down a bit faster and tried to focus on the lecturer who paced back and forth at the front of the room, probably trying to keep warm as well.

She had introduced herself as Ms Dannon and apologised for the room temperature. Evidently our former history teacher had decided not to return to the academy. I wasn't sure I blamed them. Wherever they were, it was warmer than this. Gods help us in winter.

"And that brings us to your research project for the semester." She pressed a button on her projector

—the kind normal schools used twenty or more years ago—and brought up the details. "This will all be on the website, but we can go through it all now."

I sighed and tried to focus on what she was saying. I enjoyed history, but knowing the guys were out there made it hard to concentrate.

"And so, being second years, you can choose your own study project." Ms Dannon's words got my attention.

"Anything?" I asked.

"Anything pertaining to paranormals, yes, but run it past me first." She smiled, then nodded. "All right, I'll see you next time."

"What are you thinking?" Ariana asked while we filed out of the room into the warmer air. "Please tell me you're not going to study the rise of Zeta."

I slipped my jacket off and hung it over my arm. "Why not? I know at least two hybrids."

"Neither who seem interested in talking about their upbringing," she reminded me.

I hesitated. "I suppose you're right. I could—" I was interrupted by the appearance of Matt in front of my face.

"I did not step in your way," I told him immediately.

He snorted. "Not this time, no. You're both wanted in the Chancellor's office."

"Which one?" Ariana asked.

Valid question. Unless the AMM Chancellor had resigned. Honestly, I would be surprised if my mother hadn't demanded his job after I was almost killed last year. That was precisely the kind of thing she'd do and she would probably get away with it.

"Mr Ridgeway," Matt supplied. He gestured for us to walk with him.

"Ah." So he'd kept his job. For now. Maybe no one else wanted it. Paranormals with the credentials to run a tertiary institution must be few and far between. I added that to my list of ambitions. "They gave him an office in the mansion?"

"They couldn't very well..." Matt stopped and sighed. "Yes, I suppose they could. It's on the ground floor, though."

"Right. No fancy view of the grounds. Are you his assistant now?"

"That's what I was wondering," Ariana said. "Shouldn't you be in class, too?"

"Yes," he replied dryly. "I'm trying to help clean up the mess from yesterday. And last year. The repercussions... It doesn't matter, just hurry up." He walked faster and I had to almost trot to keep up.

"What repercussions?" I asked as we drew closer.

"Having a campus here, for one thing," he replied tersely. "The Paranormal Council is hunting for a suitable alternative. They're also dealing with different factions. Some want to..." He stopped outside a door and knocked.

"Some want to what?" I asked.

When he pushed the door open, I knew I wouldn't get an answer. Not now anyway.

"Come in." Mr Ridgeway looked tired. He had more grey in his hair than he'd had when I saw him last, and more lines around his eyes. He must be around my parents' age, but he looked older.

He only drew my eye for a moment though, until I saw a figure huddled under a blanket on a chair opposite the chancellor.

"Kane!" I hurried to embrace him and kiss his mouth as he stood. Judging by the way he held the blanket with one hand, he was still naked underneath it.

Hashtag shifter life. Under other circumstances, it might be funny. Not today, though.

"Where is Dyson?" I leaned back to look into his eyes.

Tears shone and he blinked until they trickled down his cheeks. "Zeta has him." He sniffed.

My heart sank. "They… Is he…" I swallowed hard.

"He was alive when I saw him last," Kane whispered.

My head spun and I felt faint. Zeta didn't tend to keep shifters alive, from what everyone had told me. They couldn't siphon off their magic, and they couldn't breed a male in the same way they could with a woman.

"How?" I whispered.

He shook his head. "They surrounded him. Shot him with a tranquilliser dart, or something…" He leaned against my shoulder and sobbed a couple of times.

I glanced toward Matt. "We shouldn't have left."

"If we hadn't, we would have been taken too," he replied.

"We might not." I looked away from him and held Kane tight.

"Kane has suggested you could help him to get settled here," Ridgeway said after an uncomfortable silence.

"Of course. I'll show him where the uniforms are." I grimaced.

"Here's your room assignment and classes."

Ridgeway handed him a sheet of paper and a new phone. "I assume you've misplaced yours?"

Kane smiled slightly. "Yeah, it's back in the city with my car. It's probably been towed by now. Thanks."

Ridgeway nodded and waved us out. Only Matt stayed behind. I didn't bother to ask why. I doubted he'd tell me anyway.

I gripped Kane's hand and led him around to the uniform storeroom.

"So what's the plan?" I asked.

"Matt said he'd meet us in the common room after dinner," Kane said, his voice low.

"What?" Ariana asked. "Why?"

I frowned at her for a moment. "Because we're going after Dyson."

She formed an O with her mouth. "Isn't that dangerous?"

"Of course, but we can't leave him with them," I replied. "If they'd wanted him dead, they wouldn't have used a tranquilliser. They must need him for something. We need to get him out before that happens." Whatever that was. It didn't bear thinking about, but Cerberus sprang to mind. Maybe they wanted a legion of magic dog soldiers. If that was the case, they'd take blood from Dyson, lots of it.

Hopefully they would need him for long enough for us to save him first.

Although, would blood be enough? I could easily picture him coming, but not in a cup and not while under duress.

I shuddered.

"Are you okay?" Kane asked softly.

"I should be asking you that," I told him. "What happened to you?"

He shrugged. "After they caught him, I followed for a while, but I got tired. I lost them when I landed in a tree, so I spent the night there, fending off possums. First thing this morning, I flew here." He looked rueful. "I might have gotten lost a time or two."

I squeezed his hand. "At least you got here." I glanced around. This would normally be where someone like Xav would appear and make derogatory remarks about Kane being unsafe because of me. I even prepared a retort, but he was nowhere to be seen. Good, I was in no mood for his bullshit.

"Yeah." Kane sighed.

"We'll find him and bring him back," Ariana said firmly. "There's no way those bastards will beat us."

"Exactly," I agreed. "Although Dyson is probably telling terrible jokes as we speak."

"Right," Kane said with a half smile. "They might let him go so they don't have to listen to him anymore."

"If anyone could make that happen, it would be him." I leaned against Kane for a moment and reminded myself that if the guys hadn't been escorting me here, they would both be safe. I should have tried to get here alone. They would have taken me instead, but they wouldn't stop until they did that anyway. Maybe Xav was right, I was a liability to everyone here.

"He might even turn up before we can plan," Ariana said. She opened the door to the storeroom and rummaged through the shelves for pants and shirts for Kane. "They don't stock underwear," she said apologetically.

He shrugged. "I'll just go commando. It wouldn't be the first time."

I forced a smile. "It really wouldn't be. He likes to let it all hang loose."

While Ariana had her back turned, he let the blanket slip and wiggled his hips. His cock flapped back and forth.

I held back a laugh. Before he pulled his pants on all the way, I ran my fingertip down his length to watch it rise.

"Tease," he mouthed.

I gave him my best innocent-but-not-that-innocent smile and took a shirt out of its bag.

"It's a shame to cover those," I said about his abs. Damn, his body was as gorgeous as the rest of him. Abs I could do washing on, a firm V that slanted down his hips like an arrow pointing to his groin.

"I'll put it on so you can take it off later," he told me.

"Count on that," I replied.

"I will," he replied. "Isn't what those skirts are for?"

I grimaced. "I don't think that was the original intention, no." Guys and their schoolgirl fetishes. If he had a thing for girls in short skirts, it was overshadowed by his thing for wanting to have sex in front of other people. Fortunately it was a thing we shared.

"Gods, I miss jeans." Ariana turned back and handed Kane a jacket. "I'll grab some for Dyson too. He's about the same size, right?"

"More or less," Kane agreed. "I'm bigger in the dick." His face was deadpan, but I smiled, remembering Dyson's fondly.

They were about the same, but I wouldn't be so mean as to say so. Let him have his moment.

"There are no socks either." Ariana handed him a pair of shoes.

"I'll make do." He sat and pulled them on, while trying to catch glimpses up my skirt. No luck there, boyo, Ariana had spare panties that fit me. They were pink, with some kind of cat slash unicorn, but they were better than nothing.

"All right." He stood. "I guess I have to go to class and pretend I'm not worried about my brother."

I gave him a hug and kept one arm around him while we headed back toward the classrooms. "If you're lucky, they will have set up a lab for you science geeks."

8

"So, what's the plan?" Ariana settled into one of the ancient but surprisingly plush chairs.

I was about to sit beside her when Kane pulled me onto his lap and sat with his hands right over my sex. I swallowed hard and resisted the urge to writhe with the warmth of his touch.

Matt flopped into a chair opposite and rubbed his face. He looked worse than I felt.

"When did you sleep last?" I asked gently.

He shrugged. "I don't know. I'll sleep after this." His mouth pressed in a tight line and I knew that was all I would get from him.

I leaned back into Kane and rested my head against his chest.

Movement in the corner of my eye caught my attention.

Hamish stuck his head into the room and smiled tentatively. "Hey, can I help?"

Matt groaned. "Who invited him?"

"I did," Ariana replied. "Come in Hamish, of course you can help."

"The more people who know about this—" Matt shot her a warning look.

"He's the only one I told. I trust him." She moved over to give Hamish space.

"You'd better be right," Matt muttered. He crossed his arms over his chest and scowled.

I was about to ask what he was waiting for when Nash stalked into the room and closed the door behind him. He had changed into track pants and a t-shirt which hugged his torso in a way that made me want to drool.

He gave me a half smile and perched on the edge of the chair beside Matt.

"For the record, I would prefer none of you were in on this," Nash said. His brow furrowed.

"If not us, then who?" Matt asked.

"I know people," Nash said tersely. "Unfortunately they're currently too far away to be much help." He ran a hand over his hair. "That leaves us.

However, if any one of you want to opt out, now is the time." He looked at each of us in turn, his attention lingering on me.

"I'm not changing my mind," Ariana said firmly.

"Me either," I agreed.

"I'm certainly not," Kane said. His fingers tightened on the inside of my thigh.

I knew it was from anxiety, but it still sent a jolt of heat to my belly. What was wrong with me that dangerous situations didn't diminish my libido? In fact, it seemed to have the opposite effect. I forced myself to stop thinking with my groin and focus. Dyson needed us right now.

"What do you want us to do?" I asked.

I saw in his eyes that he was itching to say, "Stay here, out of trouble," but knew that would get him nowhere.

"There are a few places in the city they might keep him," Nash said. "We need to find out which one it is first. We'll split up into teams and look, then come back and discuss tactics." He squinted at us. "We have two hybrids, two witches, an owl shifter and—" He raised an eyebrow at Hamish.

"Just a regular wizard, sir," Hamish replied. He looked as though he'd stepped into the lion's den, but only now realised the danger. I gave him credit for not running away. Yet. He must really care about Ariana.

"Right," Nash nodded. "Kane, you'll be good at reconnaissance, but you have no power, defensive or offensive, to speak of." That sounded harsh, but accurate. Nash was teaching him to fight the way normals did, but that wouldn't help against guns. "You'll work with me."

"Yes, sir." Kane sounded a little disappointed. He might have been hoping to be paired with me, but he was safer with a dragon. Nash wouldn't let him come to any harm.

"Ariana and Hamish, you're together."

They both looked pleased at that.

Matt looked less pleased when he realised he was paired with me. His lip curled and he gave me a quick look through half-lidded eyes.

"I'm just as thrilled as you are," I said tartly.

"I could go with Kane," Matt said. "A gargoyle hybrid is only slightly less badass than a dragon."

The corners of Nash's mouth twitched. "If I worked with Peyton, I would get distracted."

"Same here," Kane said. He ran his hand down the inside of my thigh.

"What makes you think she wouldn't distract me, too?" Matt snapped.

When I glanced at him in surprise, he snorted. "The same way a mosquito bite on the ass is distracting."

I rolled my eyes. "Maybe I should just go by myself. Or take someone friendly, like that Xav guy."

"No one is going alone," Nash said firmly. "You two have worked together twice before and lived to tell the tale. You can do it again."

"They will," Ariana said. "So Dyson can live to *wag* the tail."

I snorted with laughter.

Matt groaned, but he was holding back a smile. Even Nash looked amused.

"Yes, exactly so. I left a bag outside the door with changes of clothes. I expect UA won't want you creeping about in their uniform." Nash rose.

"Please say there's some jeans in there," I said hopefully.

Nash opened the door and tugged it inside. "See for yourself. I'll see you all tomorrow at dawn."

"We're not leaving now?" Ariana asked.

"Nothing says suspicious like us all sneaking around in the dark," Nash said dryly. "No, we'll draw less attention during the day when places are busy. The noise will cover us if we need to become invisible."

"I guess so." Ariana sighed. "I suppose we should...um...go to bed then?" She looked meaningfully at Hamish.

"Yes." He shot up out of his chair. "Bed. For, um sleep." He offered her his hand and they slipped out the door.

Matt followed closely on their heels.

"Thank you," I said to Nash as I opened the top of the bag.

He gave me a nod and Kane an envious look, then he, too, left the room. The door clicked shut behind him.

"So, I guess we should see what might fit us in here, hmm?" Kane let me up, then knelt beside the bag. "You know you're going to have to take your clothes off before you can try on anything."

"I thought I might," I replied. "So do you."

"That's awful." He grinned. "Maybe we could help each other?"

"That sounds like a good idea." I nodded slowly, then gave him a slow smile and crept closer. He wasn't wearing a jacket or a tie, so I started on his shirt buttons first.

While I teased them through the holes, one by one, he returned the favour with mine. We almost tangled arms pushing them down each other's shoulders.

I laughed and pulled off my own sleeves while he did the same with his.

He leaned forward to kiss my mouth and unhook my bra. Without breaking our lips apart, he threw it aside.

He cupped my breast while his tongue traced the outline of my lips.

He broke off and took my hand to help me to my feet. Smiling slightly, he led me over to the window. The UA mansion was bathed in darkness, except light which glowed in several windows. Anyone looking out would have a full view of us.

Kane faced me toward the window and worked my skirt and panties down my hips.

I had no idea if anyone was watching, but the idea they might be sent my heart racing. I never thought I would be an exhibitionist, but here I was. Part of me wished there was a face in the window so I knew someone saw Kane run his hands from my neck, over my breasts and down to my sex.

He parted my legs and rubbed lightly over my mound and down toward my clit.

Did I imagine seeing a figure in a window near

the top of the mansion? They stopped and looked down toward us.

Well, enjoy the show.

Kane turned me around so he faced me, but wasn't blocking too much of the window. He ran his hands all over me, while I wound my fingers around his erect cock.

He moaned, cupped my ass and lifted me so I was pressed against the wall beside the window.

"I didn't want to rush," he whispered, "but I need you."

"I need you, too," I said. "I want you inside me." Gods knew I was already wet.

No sooner had I finished speaking than he drove his cock into me.

I gasped aloud at the suddenness. After a moment I relaxed and let him push himself in deeper.

He closed his eyes and exhaled deeply for a few moments. Then, as if by some silent signal, he began to thrust with increasing rhythm.

I glanced toward the window. Whoever was watching from the mansion still stood, backlit in the glow of the light. Evidently they liked what they saw. Was it Nash? I didn't think so, but it might be easier to pretend it was. I doubted Nash would be shy. He'd watch and not hide that he was doing it.

Kane put his hand on my waist to guide me to keep the rhythm.

I put a hand to my own breast and rubbed my nipple to drive myself closer to the edge.

He moaned. "Gods, you are so hot."

"You too," I panted.

He dipped one hand between us to rub my clit in time with each stroke.

I half closed my eyes, but cast another look at our watcher. I would almost swear I saw a hand full of cock, sliding up and down as they observed. Just when I thought this couldn't get more hot, it did.

I cried out as I crested for the first time. As I was coming down, movement outside caught my eye. Someone, maybe more than one, had stopped outside to watch.

Gods, I was as aroused as ever.

Kane moved faster inside me and rubbed at the same time. "I want you to come again," he panted. "Come for me."

So he had noticed them, too.

I arched my back so they got a better view of my breasts and rock hard nipples. A bit of me wanted one of them to join us, to run their hands over me. Knowing they saw me would have to be enough.

"You too," I said, my throat in my mouth.

He moaned. "I'm going to…"

Desire rose again, almost as fast as the first time. I bucked against his hand so hard I was on the edge again in moments.

I toppled over at the same moment he grunted and came with me. He pounded a few times, then stilled as he spilled himself into me.

We fell into each other's arms then, both holding each other up so we didn't fall in a worn heap on the floor. On the edge of my consciousness I thought I heard applause, but my pulse was louder.

After a while, we lowered each other to the floor.

"Can I ask you a favour?" he asked shyly.

"Of course," I said. Right now I might give him the world if he asked. As long as he didn't ask me to choose. I wasn't ready for that.

"Can I take a photo of you?" he asked.

I smiled slowly. "Like this?" I glanced down at my naked body.

"Yes. I swear I will never send it to anyone else." He propped himself up on one elbow.

I licked my lips. No one had ever asked me for anything like this before. After a while, I nodded.

"Okay, but if it ends up online without my permission—"

"I promise it will only go on the net if you put it there," he assured me. He pulled the phone out of the back of his pants and focused on me.

I sat with my legs together, but at an angle where my breasts would be clearly visible. I blinked as the flash went off.

"Perfect," he declared, "just like you."

I doubted that, but he went a long way to making me feel sexy.

9

"I KNOW it's only been one day, but I missed jeans." I toyed with the hem of my black t-shirt and tried not to appear as if I was looking over Matt's shoulder at the building behind him.

He shrugged. "It's better than those uniforms." He was back to head-to-toe black. His eyes scanned the road behind us. No, he didn't look suspicious at all.

"What, you don't think the short skirts are cute?" I cocked my head at him.

He squinted at me. "No."

"Why not?" I pressed.

He looked uncomfortable. "They remind me of high school."

"Ah." I nodded. Did *anyone* have fond memories

of high school? "Yeah, that makes everything about a thousand times less sexy, doesn't it?"

"At least that much," he grunted. "Are you sure this is the place?"

I pulled a piece of paper from my pocket and checked the address. "Yeah, number one hundred and thirteen. I don't suppose Nash would have sent us somewhere Zeta wouldn't be?"

Matt frowned, but I knew he was thinking the same thing. "If he did…"

"You'll write him a sternly worded letter?" I suggested.

He looked surprised, then barked a laugh. "Something like that. Maybe we should go—"

"Wait," I said quickly. A gate beside the building groaned open slowly and a black SUV pulled out. "Oh look, a cliché."

Matt gave me a funny look.

"It's black," I pointed out and peered inside as subtly as I could. "Why do the bad guys always dress that way and drive cars like that? What's wrong with pink or yellow?"

"Not just the bad guys." He gestured toward his own outfit.

I arched an eyebrow at him. "Says you," I teased.

He smirked. "It's not like you're perfect."

"Thank the gods for that." I ventured a look toward the SUV. It headed down the road toward a set of traffic lights. "Should we follow it?"

"You heard Nash. We're only here to watch."

Now I gave him a full, double brow rise. "Since when did you listen to him?"

"Since…" Matt hesitated. "Since he's the leader of this…whatever this is."

"Don't tell me you're not at least tempted to follow. Or go inside those gates before they close?"

"Of course I'm tempted, but he would kill me if I got you killed or captured."

"So you only care about what he thinks?" I asked. "Not because you care about me?"

My question obviously took him by surprise. For a fraction of a second I thought I saw something in his eyes. It was gone before I could be sure I had seen anything. A moment later, his haughty mask was back.

"You're like the pesky little sister I can't ditch," he replied.

"Right." Only I was almost certain the look he gave me smouldered. There was nothing brotherly about it. Whatever though, he was still an asshole. "I'm going in anyway. You can stay here if you like."

I drew magic from a nearby tree and formed a bubble around myself.

"Peyton," he hissed. "You stupid, fucking…"

"See, I knew you cared." I grabbed his hand and pulled him inside the bubble.

"Nothing says conspicuous like two people suddenly disappearing," he growled softly.

I shrugged. "No one was looking our way." I hoped.

"Your recklessness is going to get you killed," he stated. "Or worse, get *me* killed."

"Is that your prediction?" I stepped quickly but quietly toward the gate.

"Just stating a fact," he replied. "Now will you stop talking. They'll hear us."

It was my turn to give him a sarcastic smirk. He was the one still yabbering.

He rolled his eyes and pulled me forward just as the gate started to close.

The driveway led to a yard with enough garage space for maybe ten cars. Right now it housed four, all of them black. A couple of Zeta agents, all dressed in the same style of uniform, walked back and forth, oblivious to our presence.

The door to the rear of the building stood open at the top of a short flight of steps.

I stood on my toes to peek in. A corridor led deeper inside. Nothing looked remarkable about anything here. Just your standard, garden variety evil, government-funded-organisation building.

"I'm going inside. You're staying here," Matt said in my ear.

"Not a chance," I whispered back.

He gave me a long-suffering look and sighed. "I'm not leaving you here for your safety. I want you to watch and see who comes and goes. If they move Dyson, you'll see it."

"Oh." That actually made sense, damn him. I nodded. "Fine."

He formed his own bubble, let my hand go and stepped out of mine. The relief of not having to shield two of us was immediate. It was like not knowing you're carrying a weight until it's gone.

"Stay safe," I whispered in his general direction.

"You too."

I sensed him move away and did the same. Along the line of the fence would be a safer place to be, as long as I didn't touch it. The chance of an alarm of some kind was too great.

A third agent walked down the steps leading from the building. She must have missed bumping into Matt by a hair. She made her way across to the other agents.

"Has the parcel arrived?" she asked.

"Yes, ma'am." One of the men—tall and with bright red hair—gave her a nod. He had small eyes and a narrow nose. For some reason, he immediately gave me the creeps. It was more than just his job, there was something about him.

This was also the first time I'd known they had any kind of hierarchy, but of course they would. They acted like an arm of the military. A chain of command was only normal. Who then, was at the top?

Meanwhile, what parcel were they referring to? Dyson? Someone else? An actual parcel, like an online purchase? Maybe they needed to stock up on toothpicks or toilet paper.

"It's ready to be loaded into a car, ma'am," the agent continued. He spoke as if he only barely respected her position. In this day and age there were still some men who couldn't handle a woman in command over them.

"Good," she nodded. "See to it, Agent Fitz."

I bit my lip to keep from snorting.

"Yes, ma'am." Fitz gave her a clumsy salute. If she

noticed, she didn't respond. She simply walked around the side of the building and disappeared.

Fitz squinted after her, then finally turned and trotted up the steps and out of sight. Whatever this parcel was, I assumed he was going to get it. That suspicion was confirmed a few minutes later when Fitz returned with another agent. Between them they supported Dyson. They all but dragged him down the steps toward the cars.

My heart raced.

Dyson was alive, his chest rose and fell slowly. He looked to have been drugged. If they let him, he might shift and tear their throats out. He would hate himself for it later, but that wouldn't stop him from breaking free if he could. They would know that, too, and probably kept him sedated since they caught him.

They hauled him over to one of the cars and opened the door. Together, they heaved him inside.

I winced as he grunted in pain. At least he had some awareness left.

Fitz and the other agent, a blonde with a long scar down his cheek, stepped back from the car. Blondie opened the driver's side door and got inside, while Fitz trotted back to the building and went inside.

I licked my lips. I had an idea but I didn't know who would kill me more, Matt, Nash, Kane, Ariana, or Dyson himself if I acted on it.

I hesitated only until I heard Fitz heading back, then I ran on my tiptoes and climbed into the car beside Dyson.

He leaned against the opposite door, eyes closed, a trickle of drool on his chin. He didn't look to have been harmed, but pulling him to safety would have to wait until he woke a little more.

Just as I had that thought, he cracked open an eye and peered around. Judging by the frown, he'd felt the car move slightly, but wasn't sure why.

I grimaced to myself. I wanted to reassure him, but I couldn't just yet. Blondie was too close to risk speaking, even in a whisper.

When Dyson sniffed the air a moment later, I smiled to myself. Of course he knew I was there, he was a dog shifter and knew my scent.

He hid his own smile by ducking his head down to his chin and closing his eye.

The passenger side door opened. A moment later, the car dipped when Fitz slipped into the passenger seat. Thank the gods he had. He could have sat in the back beside Dyson. If he'd done that, he would have sat on top of me. The door slammed shut.

Just a wild guess here, but that would probably have given me away.

Blondie started the engine and pressed a button which seemed to open the gate. The faster the car went, the more uneasy I felt. Not only was I in a vehicle with evil agents, I was traveling without a seatbelt on. I'm paranormal, not immortal.

We passed through the gate and headed west.

Clinging onto magic for this long was tiring, but I had no choice. I almost lost it when Dyson flopped over toward me and ended up with his head on my hand. He peered upward, but of course he saw nothing. He still smiled.

Silly me, I smiled back. I snorted softly at myself, but pushed away the self-reprimand. I had a feeling he knew my response, even if he couldn't see it. I was probably lucky it was Dyson I was with and not Kane. Kane would probably have found a way to make me come, even if it put us both in danger.

I leaned back against my seat and put a hand on Dyson's head. If I was careful, the magic wouldn't obscure any part of him. Making half of his head invisible might expose us both.

He nestled into my hand and closed his eyes. I

stroked my thumb across his hair and sighed softly. I wouldn't mind a sleep too, but I couldn't let my guard down for a moment.

Instead, I watched out the window as we wound through the streets. After a while I realised we weren't going in a straight line. Going around bends notwithstanding, this wasn't the straightest route to the west. Or north, or south… We traveled around in a wide square before we headed west again.

"Doesn't seem like anyone is following," Blondie said.

"Good," Fitz replied. "As long as those vermin fuckers can't make cars invisible, we should be fine."

Vermin fuckers? Screw you, too, asshole.

"What do they want that for anyway?" Blondie jerked his head back toward Dyson.

That? These guys really were evil.

Fitz shrugged. "Dog DNA or something. Maybe they have a bitch ready to go into heat." He chuckled.

"Ah." Blondie nodded. "Do they need to go into heat?"

Fitz shrugged. "I don't think so. We can breed them whenever we want to."

"Oh, I see. I suppose that's easier for everyone." Blondie pulled the car up at a red light.

"It's easier for us," Fitz replied. "Don't forget,

they're little more than animals anyway. Cows and sheep. They'll do as they're told, like it or not." He looked smug.

"And, if they don't like it?" Blondie asked tentatively.

"Who cares?" Fitz replied. "This is for the good of all humankind. We're making the world a better place." He actually sounded as though he believed it. "It's as much for their benefit as ours."

"Of course," Blondie said so fast I wanted to be sick. "I was just curious."

"Yeah, well, you'd be better off not to ask too many questions," Fitz advised him. Then he added, "If you don't have the stomach for this—"

"I do," Blondie said. "I know what we're doing is right. Hybrids are important to the whole world."

"Yes, they are. It would be a lot easier if—"

Whatever he was going to say was interrupted by a grinding sound coming from the roof of the car.

10

Dyson's eyes flew open.

The grinding increased, like something was trying to tear the roof off the car. A giant talon poked a hole the size of my hand half a metre from my head.

I almost lost hold of my magic as I ducked aside.

"What the fuck?" Fitz turned to look over his shoulder. He pulled out his gun and tried to aim, but Blondie swung the wheel so hard the gun almost flew out of his hand.

Another talon gouged a hole near the first. It scraped backward, taking chunks of roof and interior fabric with it.

"Get rid of the bloody thing!" Fitz growled. "Shake it off."

"I'm trying," Blondie grunted. "Can't you kill it?"

"If I can get off a shot." Fitz aimed again and squeezed the trigger. The bullet missed both talons and lodged in the roof between them.

"Bulletproof goes both ways," Dyson whispered and gave a snort.

I grinned, but joking aside, we really needed to get out of this car.

The talons tugged harder and the roof groaned. The car shuddered with the strain of being pulled in two different directions.

I held on to my magic long enough to pull my phone out of my pocket.

My sudden appearance must have caught Blondie's eye, because he glanced back and gaped before returning his attention to his driving.

"Shit!" he shouted out a moment later.

"I knew that would come in useful someday." I nodded toward the road in front of the car. A moment later we slammed into the temporary concrete and plastic waterslide I had conjured in the middle of the quiet country highway.

I cried out as I flew hard into the seat in front of me. Pain exploded through my shoulder and down my arm.

Through watering eyes I watched a scaled, black

form roll over the windscreen and down the front of the car. The dragon would have struck the water-slide, but the structure disappeared as quickly as it had come. Instead, he tumbled onto the tar in a tangle of legs and wings.

He slowly rose and shook it off before he stalked back toward the car.

"Shit," Fitz said from behind his airbag.

"We should go," I told Dyson.

He nodded and opened his door. "Are you all right?"

"Yeah." I rubbed my shoulder before I climbed across the back of the car. "Nothing broken I don't think." At least, I hoped not, but it hurt like hells.

He gave me his hand and tugged me out just as the dragon stepped up onto the front of the car.

"He looks pissed," I remarked.

"When does Nash not look pissed?" Dyson asked.

"I don't think now is the time for me to answer that," I replied.

Nash scraped at the windscreen with one huge talon and peered in at the two terrified agents.

"I think you've made your point," I told him. They would have a hard enough time explaining this acci-dent to the police. The front of the car was smashed up, but no hint of what it had struck remained. The cops wouldn't be likely to believe a waterslide had appeared out of nowhere only to disappear again. That was even more bizarre than the presence of a dragon.

Nash turned huge eyes to me and bobbed his head, but still scratched the glass one more time. The agents cowered in the car until Nash climbed down and stalked away, toward Dyson and me.

He jerked his head toward his back.

"You want us to ride you?" I asked.

Nash bobbed his huge head. Even knowing who he was, I was a little intimidated. I mean, it wasn't every day you saw a dragon in Melbourne, much less rode one.

Nash snorted out his enormous nostrils and jerked his head back.

"Okay, okay." I stepped closer. "How do I get up there? Just…climb?" He didn't disagree, so I put a hand on his warm scales and considered the best way to do this.

"Here." Dyson laced his fingers and leaned down to make a stirrup.

"Thank you." I winced as I stepped onto his hands and threw a leg over Nash's back. I settled onto his warm body and wound my arms around his neck as best I could.

"There's room for two." I assumed Nash could support us both, or at least thought he could.

"Uh, no offence," Dyson took a step back, "but I'd prefer to run." He glanced back toward the car as though he really wanted to rip the agent's heads off. Under the circumstances, I applauded his restraint.

He shed his Zeta prisoner attire, shifted into his wolfhound form, and stood with his tongue lolling out of the side of his mouth. No doubt about it, he was cute in both his forms.

Nash spread his wings just as Fitz managed to work his way past the airbag and mangled car. He staggered onto the road and raised his gun.

"Hold it right there," he ordered. "Don't so much as twitch or I'll shoot."

I turned my arm so my tattoo was upward and readied myself to bring my guardian to life.

Before I could act, another gargoyle leapt onto the back of the car. He jumped from the roof onto Fitz and knocked him clear off his feet. The gun flew out of his hand and spun across the tar.

Dyson ran for it, picked the weapon up in his jaws and disappeared into the bushes.

Matt stood over Fitz and growled deeply, his muzzle a handspan from the agent's face.

Fitz's eyes widened in terror. A puddle formed on the road around his pants.

Yeah, I would have wet myself too, if I thought a gargoyle might rip my throat out.

Matt looked toward us and jerked his head upward. The message was clear: get out of here.

Nash bobbed his head and with a stroke of his wings, we were airborne and hovering over the wreck.

Another car approached from the east.

I held my breath until Matt bounded away in the direction Dyson had gone.

Nash banked hard and took us both toward the shelter of the trees.

I didn't envy Fitz and Blondie having to explain all of this to whoever arrived on the scene next. That was their problem. Maybe they shouldn't have chosen the wrong side. Although, I had a niggling doubt in the back of my mind that Blondie had. He didn't seem convinced what he was doing was right.

I gave myself a mental shrug. He wouldn't have been merciful to me had he known I was there. I owed him nothing in return.

Sirens in the distance suggested someone had called the police or an ambulance.

That led to another thought.

"Nash, would they have—"

I squealed when he dropped several metres. I slipped to one side a little before I managed to catch myself. A fall from this height would suck.

"What are you— Fuck!"

A form few right over my head. Had Nash not seen and dropped the way we had, the phoenix would have snatched me off his back. I'd be a snack as we spoke.

"Have I mentioned I don't like phoenixes?" I cried out.

Nash snorted his agreement and dropped lower, so we wove between the trees, barely off the ground. If I had ever envisioned flying on the back of a dragon, it wouldn't have been like this.

I leaned further forward and gripped him tighter. One slip and things might end badly for me.

I screwed my eyes shut and sat like that for a solid minute or two. My breakfast threatened to rise. Only the idea that I might puke on Nash made me reopen my eyes.

The trees passed by in a blur.

I glanced over my shoulder.

The phoenix, feathers a stunning shade of blue, was right behind us. He'd be beautiful if he wasn't trying to kill us.

"I guess that answers my question on whether or not they called for backup," I said ironically.

Nash banked suddenly. Over my shoulder I spied another phoenix.

"Crap. I don't suppose there's any chance that one is on our side?"

That question was answered a moment later when the second phoenix gave chase.

"Well shit," I muttered. Hanging on for dear life with one hand, I pulled out my phone and clicked on the spell app Madame Luc had taught us to use. I pushed away a pang of grief for the teacher who had died defending the academy last year, and scrolled.

"Magpie? Too small? Goat? Too on-the-ground." Unless the phoenixes got hungry. "Elephant? Let's call that plan B. Oh, this wasn't here last year." I grinned to myself, pointed my phone over my shoulder and clicked as I drew magic from the trees to put into the spell.

The pterodactyl appeared with an ear-piercing shriek and dove straight at the first phoenix. The hybrid never stood a chance. Clearly he hadn't antic-ipated anything appearing in front of him, much less a carnivorous, winged dinosaur.

I winced at the crunch of prehistoric teeth on

bone. The phoenix hit the ground a few moments later, without his head.

I swallowed hard and glanced back as the second phoenix evaded the pterodactyl.

"Damn," I muttered, and again when the phoenix narrowly missed slamming into a tree.

I scrolled through my phone again for something else I could conjure. Snake, hippopotamus, bicycle—that sounded like a crash waiting to happen—table, chair… Nothing which could fly or was capable of defending us against the big hybrid.

We flew low until I caught sight of Dyson and Matt. Both stood under the shelter of a tree, their eyes raised toward us.

I didn't realise what Nash intended until he hit the ground with a jerk that pulled my grip free. I rolled over the side of his wing and landed in the ground with a thud. I cried out with pain—of course had I landed on my already hurt arm.

"What the fuck, you—" I wasn't even on my feet before Nash was off again, phoenix in his wake, the pterodactyl right behind. "Bloody idiot," I muttered.

"Peyton!" Dyson, back in human form and deliciously naked, came running toward me. "We need to get you out of here."

"Hey, who was rescuing who?" I retorted.

Matt growled. I'm sure that was directed at Dyson or Nash. I totally hadn't ditched him back in the city to jump into the car. Nope, not me. Okay, so I had, but he didn't need to growl about it now.

"Look." Dyson pulled me under a tree and pointed.

Unencumbered by my weight, Nash turned in mid-air and raked his enormous talons in the direction of the phoenix.

That slowed the hybrid long enough for the pterodactyl to catch up. It screeched and fastened its own claws into the phoenix's back.

The phoenix gave a very human-like scream and writhed to escape from the pterodactyl's grip.

The dinosaur held fast, then shook the phoenix until a loud snap rent the air.

I grimaced as the phoenix sagged.

A second later my spell ended and the pterodactyl disappeared. The dead phoenix fell from the sky and landed with a ground-shaking thump.

"What a way to go," Dyson muttered.

"Yeah." I leaned against the tree trunk and tried not to spew. Who else would die before this was over?

"I think we're late for class," Dyson added.

I laughed. It started soft, but ended up sounding

hysterical. We were late, but at least we had Dyson back. I stopped laughing for long enough to look into his eyes. What had they done to him? Whatever it was, I would pay them back for it some day. All of that and more.

But first, I needed a drink.

I nodded to the west. "The academy is that way. You're going to love the uniforms."

What a horrible way to cover a perfectly good dick.

11

Nash gave me a look that left me somewhere between wet panties and wanting to hide behind the chair.

"What were you thinking?" he growled.

I returned his glare without flinching. "I was thinking Dyson needed help to escape," I replied evenly. "The chance presented itself and I took it. How did you know where to find me anyway?"

"I saw them take Dyson out of the building," Matt said. "They put him in the car and left. When I couldn't find you, I figured you'd done something stupid." He gave me a scathing look.

I narrowed my eyes at him, but heat rose up my cheeks. "Dyson needed my help."

"Yes, Dyson did," Dyson agreed. "Without Peyton,

the car wouldn't have crashed. Well, not like that." He turned to me. "Good job, by the way."

"Thank you." At least someone appreciated me.

"Thank you for helping my brother." Kane sat beside me on the couch and squeezed my hand.

"We would have managed perfectly well without her," Matt said darkly. "Nash could have just pulled the roof off the car and grabbed Dyson. You were there to help *find* Dyson, that was all."

"Right," I replied, "and there's no way you would have done what I did, hmmm?" I stared him down until he glanced away.

"For what it's worth, I think Peyton is very brave," Ariana declared. "If I had been there, I probably would have peed my pants."

Hamish nodded his agreement.

I shot them a grateful smile. "I might have almost done that." After a moment I sighed deeply. "All right, fine. I admit jumping into the car wasn't the smartest thing to do, but it seemed right at the time."

"Did it ever occur to you," Nash said, his tone menacingly soft, "that the whole thing was a trap to draw you in?"

It hadn't. It should have. The blood drained out of my face and I swallowed.

"Of course not," I said after a while. "You wouldn't have sent me there if it was."

His eyebrow quirked upward. "Never assume." He knew I was right though, I saw it in his eyes. He had chosen the safest place to send me. He and Kane had gone to the most dangerous. Only, he had miscalculated. Or had he?

"What did you find?" I asked bluntly. "Where you went. What was so terrible you had to risk yourself?" If he or Kane had gotten hurt, I would have been devastated. My heart ached at the very idea. Would any of them mind if I locked us all away somewhere Zeta couldn't find us?

Of course they would. None of the guys would let Zeta stop them from living their lives.

Nash looked away, toward the window. The same window where, just last night, Kane and I had…put on a show.

I swallowed hard at the memory. "Nash." My voice squeaked a little. "What did you find?"

He exhaled heavily. "It was…"

"It was empty," Kane finished for him. "Whatever they had been doing there, they're gone now."

"Empty is better than—" I paused. "Wait, you think they knew you were coming?" For some reason, my gaze went to Matt.

His face reddened and he scowled. "If you're thinking I told them, you can fuck off right now."

"No, I know you didn't," I said quickly. He had risked his life over and over. If he worked for Zeta, he wouldn't have done that. "Nash, you thought someone told them about where the academy was when it was in Sydney?"

Nash nodded slowly. "The only people who knew about our excursion are in this room." He scrutinised everyone. "Hamish, how did you come to be here with us?"

While Hamish's face turned white, Ariana sat forward in front of him.

"He's with me," she said firmly. "I trust him."

"Can we trust you?" Nash asked.

"Yes, you can!" Ariana's eyes shone with tears. "All I've wanted here was to help, and to keep Peyton safe."

"She's on our side," Matt said firmly. "Her aunt is on the council. Has it occurred to anyone, maybe Dyson didn't get caught?"

"What the fuck, man?" Dyson shook his head. "You can't be implying what I *think* you are?"

"I watched him get caught," Kane said, his face pink with fury. "My brother would never—"

"What about *you* then?" Matt asked.

Kane launched himself out of his chair toward Matt.

Nash was faster. He leapt up and caught Kane's shoulders and held him back.

"Let me go," Kane growled. "I'm going to deck the motherfucker."

"That's what I'm afraid of," Nash said, more calm than I would have been under the circumstances. "We don't need to resort to violence. Matt, Kane, and Dyson, I trust you all implicitly or you wouldn't be allowed in Peyton's company."

Now it was my turn to get angry. "You don't get to decide who I spend time with."

Nash stepped back from Kane and fixed me with an unapologetic look. "If I knew they were working with Zeta, getting expelled from the academy would be the least of their worries."

I swallowed. I had no doubt he meant what he said. If anyone betrayed us, Nash might just bite their heads off.

He glanced around the room. "Consider that a warning. Neither I nor the council have patience for spies, especially ones who would lead to any of us ending bac...ending up in a Zeta laboratory. Understood?"

"Yes, sir," I replied.

He gave me a smouldering look, then glared at Hamish and Ariana before he took his seat again.

Kane flopped down beside me. I put an arm around his shoulder and leaned into him.

"Are you all right?" I asked softly.

He glanced toward Matt. "Yeah. I just don't like anyone casting aspersions on my brother."

Matt shrugged. "Sorry, I guess. Emotions are high right now."

"Yeah." Kane gave me a squeeze, then locked his gaze on mine. "Yeah they are." The look in his eyes turned from anger to desire.

I raised my eyebrows. I knew exactly what he was thinking. Right here, in front of all these people?

He gave me a nod and dipped his mouth down toward mine. He slipped his arms around my neck and let his tongue dance with mine.

"I guess we're done here," Matt remarked. I thought he might get up and leave then, but he didn't. Fine, he couldn't blame me for anything he saw.

Kane pulled his mouth from mine and kissed his way down my cheek to my neck.

"If you don't want to watch, you should leave," he said, his voice muffled. "But we don't mind if you stay."

I murmured my agreement. It turned into a moan as he cupped my breast and rubbed his palm over my nipple.

Ariana and Hamish snuck out of the room. I assumed they had their own plans.

From the corner of my eye I saw Dyson stand, too. I assumed he was leaving. I was disappointed, but I understood. Instead, he moved toward the door, locked it and returned to his seat.

Well then.

Kane lay me back on the couch and kissed my mouth while he tugged my shirt up off my breasts.

I flushed slightly, but at this point I dared not look at anyone. Knowing they watched excited me enough to almost make me come on the spot. I sat up just enough to pull off my t-shirt and drape it over the arm of a chair.

When I lay back down, Kane crouched beside me, his body angled so as to not block the view too much. He kissed my mouth, my jaw and down my chest to claim a nipple between his lips.

I groaned softly and turned my face. I caught sight of Matt, his eyes wide, hand on the bulge in his pants. Nash sat with a raised eyebrow, but he seemed to have forgotten how to blink.

I turned my attention back to Kane and helped

him out of his shirt before he undid my jeans and worked them down my hips. I kicked them off while he ran his fingers over the front of my panties.

"You're amazing," he said softly.

I smiled. I wasn't sure if I was that amazing, but I knew this was pretty much his wildest wet dream coming true, right here.

"So are you," I replied. "I want you."

He licked his lips and hooked his fingers into the sides of my panties. In one motion, he had them down my legs to my feet. I kicked them aside.

"Sit up a bit," he said, breathless. He took my arm and leaned me against the side of the couch. He knelt beside me and parted my legs with his hands, opening me up for everyone to see.

If you'd told me a year ago I would want to do this, I would have laughed. Now, I wanted it very, very much. I half closed my eyes, but left them open enough to see Matt's hand disappear down the front of his track pants. Nash watched with interest, hands crossed over his chest. Dyson's face was unreadable, but he didn't look away.

Kane slipped a finger inside me, then another. In full view of everyone, he thrust in deep. He rubbed the heel of his hand against my clit while his fingers massaged my g-spot. With his other hand, he rolled my nipple between his thumb and forefinger.

I bucked against his hand, well aware my breasts rose and fell with each movement.

"I'm going to come," I said loud enough for everyone to hear.

"Come for me," Kane urged. "Come for *us*."

That was enough to push me over the edge. I crested hard, but left room for more.

Kane pulled his fingers out of me and removed his jeans and boxer shorts. He frowned for a moment, then sat on the couch and pulled me onto his lap, facing away from him. His hands on my hips, he guided me down onto his cock.

I moaned as he filled me. I almost lost it again at the look on Dyson's face. He watched my whole body rise and fall as Kane helped me ride him.

I held out a hand toward Dyson. I didn't want to pressure him. I knew he wanted me, and preferred to take things slowly. I respected that, but I wanted him to touch me, too.

He hesitated, then took my hand and moved over slowly to kneel beside me. Almost reverently, he cupped one breast, then the other. He rubbed my hard peaks, then replaced his hands with his mouth.

He licked and sucked my nipples like a man who hadn't eaten in days.

His hand slipped down between my legs and rubbed my clit in time with his brother's thrusts.

I moaned loudly. Between them both, I was hotter than I could ever imagine.

"Dyson," I whispered.

He looked me in the eyes and licked his lips.

I gave him a quick nod.

He rose and pushed his track pants down his hips to expose his rock-hard erection. He cupped my cheek with his hand and eased his cock into my mouth.

The groan I heard this time was from Matt. His eyes looked glazed and he wasn't even trying to hide that he was pleasuring himself. That only drove me wilder still. I remembered my fantasy on the bus about Nash's mouth on Matt's cock, but Nash hadn't moved.

I closed my eyes and teased the tip of Dyson's cock with my tongue.

He panted and wound his hand through my hair. "Gods, woman, your mouth is…" He panted again.

I sucked hard and reached up to massage his balls.

He thrust between my lips. His hand held me tight.

Somehow both brothers moved in perfect synch. Having both of them inside me at once drove me hard and fast toward the edge and over. As I came again, I wondered what it would be like to have Nash or Matt in my rear hole. That made me come for a third time.

Kane grunted and thrust harder before he too came. Dyson was a moment behind him, his hot cum filling my mouth.

I sagged back against Kane and let Dyson slide himself loose.

"Wow," Kane breathed.

I murmured my agreement. "We should do this again sometime."

"Definitely." Dyson sat beside us and lightly rubbed the back of his hand over my nipples. "Sometime soon."

"So, your boyfriends got back alive, huh? How many died for that?"

I turned off my phone and glanced over my shoulder. "What do you want, Xav?"

He flopped down beside me. "You know what I want."

I sighed. "I'm not leaving until the rest of the AMM leaves too."

"I'm sure that could be arranged," he said dryly.

"Again with the threats." I crossed my arms over my chest. My gargoyle tattoo was clearly visible. He eyed it with what looked like amusement. This from a guy who had—I glanced over. Damn, he wore long sleeves. If he had any kind of guardian, I couldn't see it. Hells, for all I knew, he might be a shifter. Probably a lame one, like a flea.

"I told you before, it's not a threat," he said coolly. "But that's actually not what I'm here for."

Don't ask, don't ask, don't—

"What *are* you here for?"

Damn it, Peyton.

"I want to challenge you to a duel." He watched me through half-lidded eyes.

"A duel? As in, pistols at dawn?"

He chuckled. "Nothing that barbaric. I meant a magical duel. I'm a wizard, you're a witch. Neither of us is a hybrid."

"You assume."

"I know," he said firmly.

"For someone who doesn't like me, you seem to know a lot about me."

"I make it a point to know my enemy."

I raised my eyebrows. "Enemy? That's a bit dramatic, don't you think?"

"Not at all. It's the name I give to anyone who might get me killed."

"Ahhh." I nodded. "I would call them Zeta."

"If you don't leave, they could kill us all." His eyes darkened.

"If I leave, they still might," I pointed out.

"If they do, it will be because you led them here."

I leaned toward him, almost nose to nose. "I can assure you, with absolute certainty that I did not." I sat back. "Mr Nash surmised there was a mole in the academy. Someone who is working for them."

"So you brought that mole here?" His eyes snapped.

"Not me personally, no," I said as calmly as I could. "The UA administration invited us. If you're looking for someone to blame, maybe you should start there."

My words hit home, I saw it on his face. He sat back and rubbed his chin.

"Go onto Twitter and rant," I suggested, fully knowing he couldn't.

He curled his lip at me. "I still want you and yours gone. In the meantime, my offer of a duel stands."

"Are we allowed to duel?" I asked.

"Of course not," he said lightly.

"Let me guess, if we get caught, we get thrown out?" I cocked my head at him.

"We won't get caught."

"I'm sure you'll make sure *you* don't get caught."

He narrowed his eyes. "Whatever you might think of me, I don't cheat. I want you gone, but I'm not going to set you up to do it."

"I'm supposed to buy that?" I asked. "To be honest, it sounds like the perfect way to ruin my life."

He considered for a moment. "You're right, it does, but that's not how I roll. Duels have rules we both have to follow."

"Let me guess. If you win, I leave."

He nodded.

"And if I win, what then?"

He smirked. "You won't."

"Cocky bastard, aren't you?" I rolled my eyes. He was at least as annoying as Matt, without the mysterious gargoyle shifter thing to make him more appealing.

"I know my own abilities," he said. "If you win, I'll back off."

"How about you just back off?" I suggested. "Surely you have better things to do than bother me every day?"

"You'd think so, wouldn't you," he agreed. "But I'm driven. I won't stop until UA is safe again."

For a moment I seriously considered getting up and walking away. Not just from him but from the academy. I could study teaching at a normal university. Maybe one out of reach of Zeta. Was there a university in the South Pole? Everyone could get on with their lives without me to put them in danger.

I almost laughed out loud at myself. Zeta wouldn't give up. As long as they and I existed, they would be after me. More than that, they would be after every paranormal on and off campus. Whatever they wanted Dyson for, they would still need him or some other dog shifter.

This whole thing was much, much bigger than me.

I shook my head. "I would need something more when I win. More than you leaving me alone." I rubbed my forehead. A headache was threatening at the edges of it. "What about a favour you can't refuse?"

He knitted his brows. "What kind of favour?"

I shrugged. "I don't know. If you're so sure you'll win, there's no risk of you having to worry about it, is there?"

He nodded slowly. "That's true." He stuck his hand out to me. "I'll see you out on the running field at ten pm."

"What, not midnight?" I eyed his hand before I shook it.

"No reason not to hold it at a civilised hour." He

held my hand a few moments too long before he let it go and stood. "You can bring two others. One to peel you off the grass when we're done and one as a judge. Your judge and mine will confer and decide on a winner if it's not too obvious. You know, when you run away screaming."

I laughed. "As if that will happen."

He shrugged with one shoulder. "You say that now." He took a few steps away before he turned back. "Oh, and no teachers."

"Why would I bring one of them?" I asked, trying to keep any thoughts off my face.

He regarded me for a long moment, as if attempting to figure something out. "No reason," he said finally. He gave a curt nod and walked away.

I was almost certain he didn't know anything about Nash and me. Perhaps he *thought* he knew, and had been hoping to catch me off guard. He'd have to try harder than that. I was always on the lookout for anyone who might ask about him and any relationship we might have. Still, knowing Xav was suspicious was a good reason to be extra careful. I doubted he'd pull any punches when it came to anyone from AMM, teacher or student.

"What did he want?" Dyson flopped down on the grass beside me. Kane joined us a moment later.

I told them about the duel and the deal Xav and I had made.

"Do you think I'm crazy for agreeing to it?" I gave them a tentative look.

Kane returned it with a lopsided smile. "It's not as if you'll lose." He sounded so confident I almost believed him.

"I might," I replied.

"You won't." Dyson leaned in to kiss my mouth lightly. "You'll leave him all over the grass out there." He waved toward the running field.

I chewed my lip. "I hope so, or I'm out."

"If you're out—" Kane started.

I pressed my fingertips to his lips. "Don't say it. You need to be here. Both of you. What you guys want to do with your lives, you can't learn at a normal university. You belong here."

"We could defer until AMM has a different campus," Kane said. He and Dyson exchanged glances.

"Right, we could," Dyson agreed.

"We could have done that to start with," I pointed out. "If we did, then Zeta wins. Or the UA brats win. Either way, someone else is deciding things for us. Why let that happen? We have as much right to be here as anyone else."

"And that's why you'll win," Dyson said. "But you should see Matt before you do anything else."

"Why?" No doubt Matt would call me a bloody fool for even thinking of accepting the challenge. Who was I kidding? He would take any excuse he could find to lecture me on whatever failing I had that day.

Dyson gave me an adorable lop-sided smile which made my heart skip. He really was so stinking cute. Both twins were.

"Because," Dyson said slowly, "he can add a few more tattoos to your arm."

My eyebrows shot up. "Is that allowed?"

Dyson shrugged. "I don't see why not. Xav has kept his collection close to his chest, so to speak."

"Right." I remembered his long sleeves. They could be hiding almost anything. I hadn't even seen an outline under the fabric.

"Without knowing what you're up against, you have to be ready for anything," Kane concluded.

"Exactly." Dyson nodded. "He might have a giant reptile tattooed on himself."

"You think he might fight with Godzilla?" I asked. What a cliché that would be.

Dyson grinned. "Why not? I know I would."

"He really would," Kane agreed. "He's been obsessed with Godzilla since we were kids."

"I always preferred King Kong myself," I replied, "but no judgement either way. I mean, better those than Mothra." I grinned at the look on Kane's face. "Don't tell me, you're a Mothra guy?"

He shrugged. "At least Mothra could fly."

"True." I half switched off as the guys chatted about various superheroes and monsters they enjoyed or reading about. I love a good monster or superhero movie, but my mind was on the duel.

Honestly, I had a better idea of what Zeta might throw at me than Xav. Phoenixes, griffins, jerks with guns. Xav might have—the gods knew what. I would need to have something up my sleeve. As much as I didn't want to admit it, that meant asking Matt for help. He would probably have a much better idea about all of this than I did.

I sighed to myself. Undoubtedly he'd give me all the information I needed, while telling me off the whole time for getting involved in something I shouldn't.

And getting him involved.

And—

"Wouldn't you agree?" Kane asked. He draped an arm over my shoulder.

"With what?" I asked, confused.

Dyson chuckled. "I told you she wasn't listening."

I socked Dyson playfully on the arm. "Maybe you two should get more tattoos, too."

Kane looked thoughtful. "Of what? A unicorn like Ariana?" A grin tugged at the corners of his mouth.

I smiled slightly in return. "Sure, why not, that would be cute. Rainbow mane and all. Although, I think you'd suit pink better."

Dyson laughed. "I dare you."

Kane grimaced. "Not a chance. Unless you do it first."

Dyson held up his hands. "No way. A Pegasus maybe. A black one, with a streak of red in its mane."

"That would be cool," Kane agreed. "We could all get one."

I wondered if all would include Nash. If so, where would he have it? Somewhere no one would see it but me, most likely. Maybe his ass.

I licked my lips at *that* visual image. I would happily run the tip of my tongue over his taut skin and…

"Come on, let's go and find Matt." Kane stood and offered me his hand.

Dyson did the same a moment later.

I grabbed a hand in each of mine and let them pull me to my feet. Hand in hand, we walked back toward the academy building, a growing sense of unease in my belly.

This duel could go badly, very badly.

13

"THE RULES ARE," Xav's friend Gunter regarded all of those gathered with the same disdain, even Xav, "no deadly hand to hand combat. No conventional weapons like guns and knives. The combatant must recall any creature they create prior to the death of their opponent. Failure to do the latter will award the victory to the opponent."

I grimaced. Winning wouldn't be much use if one was dead.

"They don't usually end in death," Matt said helpfully.

I eyed him sideways. Once I'd told him what was going on and he'd finished telling me I was an idiot, he had insisted on being my judge. If anyone would be impartial, it would be him. He knew what I had at stake, but he wouldn't make a ruling in my favour just because we were…whatever we were to each other. Friends, maybe, in spite of sharing a kiss. Friends with sexual attraction. That was frustrating, but undeniable.

"Usually?" I asked.

He shrugged. "Accidents happen. Don't worry, that won't happen here, I'll make sure of it."

"Are you trying to say you care?" I asked, giving him a half smile.

He arched an eyebrow and gave me a look which I couldn't quite interpret. Something which suggested his feelings for me ran deeper than he let on, or wanted to admit to himself.

My eyes locked on his. Warmth traveled through me. It was more than sexual attraction. I had come to care for him, even though he drove me crazy. Maybe *because* he did. At least life wasn't dull with him around.

He broke the contact first.

"Of course not, but I'd get my head bitten off if I let you come to any harm," he said easily.

He didn't need to say who would do the biting. We both knew Nash would be furious if anything happened to me.

"I'd peck his eyes out," Kane said with a nod

toward Matt. He and Dyson had played rock, paper, scissors to determine which of them would accompany Matt and I. As consolation, Dyson would take me out to dinner. I guess that meant I won either way, as long as I didn't lose the duel.

"Of course you would." Matt shot Kane a flat look. "If you could catch me to do it."

Kane grinned. "I could wait until Dyson had you pinned down first."

Whatever Matt thought of that, he didn't get the chance to say.

Gunter cleared his throat loudly and gestured toward the field in the middle of the running track.

"Duellers, take your places."

Matt gave me a wave to move to my designated spot—a line of paint sprayed on the grass. It glowed softly, but would fade in daylight so no one would know what we'd been up to.

Xav swaggered to his line and curled his lip at me. "A little overdressed, aren't you?"

I cocked my head at him. "Huh?"

He smirked. "I hear you like to put on a show. At least you'll have a career as a porn star when this is over."

I hoped the darkness hid my blush. "That's your

angle? Slut shaming? You'll have to try harder than that."

He grinned. "I bet you say that to all the guys."

I shrugged. "Not really. My lovers know what they're doing. Do I sense some insecurity in that department?"

His smile faded. "No. I'm fully secure in my manhood."

"Sure you are." I nodded slowly. "Are we going to do it or not?"

"We're not…" He spluttered before he must have realised what I was actually referring to.

I smiled. In the corner of my eye I saw Matt and Kane laughing. Even Xav's support, a woman named Kylie, looked to be chuckling.

I was so distracted I almost missed Xav's arm shoot up. Magic poured out the end, to land on the grass in front of me. Before it could even form into anything cohesive, I threw up a bubble of magic around myself and went invisible.

"Cheat," Xav hissed.

"There's no rule against it." I ran several steps to the side as a giant snake appeared on the grass. It hissed and looked around itself, tongue out as if to taste the air.

What did I know about snakes? Didn't they sense vibrations? I stomped my foot on the ground. The snake's head swung toward the sound. I tiptoed away so when the snake slid over and struck, it touched only air.

How was its eyesight? I dropped my bubble and gave it a wave. No response. Well then, I could conserve some energy.

I tiptoed further away while Xav grumbled under his breath. I dearly wanted to strike back, but Matt and I had discussed my plan—okay, he'd told me what I needed to do to turn the odds in my favour, but it made sense.

With a faint pop, the snake disappeared. Xav stalked toward me, his brow creased in a scowl. He looked like he wanted to aim a blast of magic at me and end this here and now. He didn't. He must have known killing me would probably result in him getting kicked out of UA.

That, and I didn't believe he wanted me dead. No, he wanted to humiliate me and beat me fair and square. He wanted to watch me leave the academy grounds, my lovers a step behind me. In this scenario, he wanted to be some kind of hero.

What an asshole.

"That the best you've got?" I taunted. "Your snake?

It was a bit small, wasn't it? Not very efficient, either."

Xav gave me an ugly smile. "I figured you'd stop and suck it. I bet you'd like it deep down the back of your throat."

"Again with you projecting your thoughts onto me." I clicked my tongue. "Have you ever considered therapy?"

"Since I met you I have," he said.

I shook my head. "And they say sex addiction isn't rcal."

"As if I'd fuck you," he sneered.

"Right back at you," I told him. I watched his body carefully so when he raised his arm again, I was ready.

An enormous spider appeared on the grass a couple of metres away.

I shuddered.

"Scared of a little spider?" Xav taunted.

Little spiders, no. There was nothing small about this thing. Or its…were they teeth? Fangs?Whatever, they looked wicked sharp.

It turned toward me and started forward on all eight, hairy limbs. It scurried faster than I would have thought anything that big could move.

I struck out with a blast of magic when it was barely a hand's length away.

Magic struck the creature on the front of its head and made it recoil. It threw up its front two legs as if to ward off another blow.

I might have felt sorry for the spider, but it wasn't real. For a bug created by magic, it was impressive, even though it was creepy as hells.

I took a few steps back.

The spider lowered its front legs and matched me step for step.

I thought I heard Xav snicker. I assumed he was ready to call off the spider the moment it had me pinned, ready to bite. That would give him the win, probably in record time.

He wished.

I aimed another blast of magic, but this one landed behind the spider.

Xav barked a laugh, but the spider turned toward the gouge in the grass, its attention drawn long enough for me to direct a long blast toward the middle of its body.

The spider shuddered, then popped out of existence.

Xav swore. The spider was replaced by a bear.

I made myself invisible and ducked just before a

claw swiped past my head. That would have taken off my face if I hadn't been so quick. Matt had been right, Xav was getting angry and sloppy.

The bear growled. Any louder and it might have woken the academy. So much for secrecy.

It turned and sniffed the air, reminding me of the Zeta agent I'd nicknamed Cerberus.

I backed up a few more paces. It followed, tracking my scent.

A waterslide might be handy right now, to distract the bear. Maybe with enough water, it would wash away. I had considered asking Matt to tattoo one on my arm, but decided against it on the grounds it would look bizarre. I wanted to defend myself, not look like an idiot while I did it.

I caught sight of Xav, arms crossed over his chest, a cocky expression on his face. He was obviously convinced the bear would hunt me down and pin me. It might do the first, but I wouldn't let it do the second.

I circled around behind Xav, until he was between the bear and me. I dropped the bubble of magic and waved my arms in the air.

"Hey, over—"

Xav must have anticipated the move. He spun and shot off a blast of magic. Perfectly contained for maximum punch without being deadly, it threw me off my feet.

I flew back several metres and hit hard enough to knock the wind out of me.

I lay stunned as Kane shouted for me to get up.

"Peyton! The bear!"

Fuck.

I rolled in time to avoid missing a paw that would have pressed me to the ground. It was a much more controlled manoeuvre than the initial paw swipe. That suggested Xav managed to draw back his emotions somewhat.

The bear stumbled forward and almost fell. Before it hit the ground, it disappeared.

Xav growled and aimed another blast of magic at me, but missed. Apparently his emotions were volatile.

Good.

I jumped to my feet and blasted Xav with my own magic. He jumped aside with more agility than I would have expected for someone of his size, and shot back.

I nimbly sidestepped.

If I was going to do something, it would have to be soon.

He came at me again, with blast after blast. Each

one got slightly weaker than the one before. He was starting to tire. The effort of creating the magical beasts had started to tell on him.

Just as Matt said it would.

"He's an arrogant hothead," Matt has explained while he inked my arm. "He'll try to throw everything at you in the hope of overpowering you quickly. Hold him off and let him wear himself out. Then you can go at him with everything you have. And this—this will do the trick."

I raised my wrist. In striking detail, like all of Matt's work, the tiger stood ready to strike. Silent, precise, powerful…or so I hoped.

The big cat leapt off my arm and stalked Xav. He backed away, eyes wide, even though he must have known the big cat couldn't kill him. Or at least, it wouldn't.

He jumped to the side as the tiger leapt. It landed lightly and twisted, immediately continuing the hunt.

Xav raised trembling hands and blasted the tiger on the chest.

The tiger let out a soft growl and faltered slightly.

Xav grinned and blasted it again. "Is this your secret weapon, bitch?" he taunted. "It's a bit useless."

"Not as useless as yours," I replied. I focused on

the tiger, reinforcing it so when it swiped at Xav with its paw, the blow was careful and aimed well enough to knock him off his feet.

Xav let out a squeak as the tiger pounced. It pinned him to the ground with an enormous paw.

"Judges!" I beckoned them over.

Matt was grinning.

Gunter still looked bored. "It's clear, the winner is—"

Xav blasted the tiger in the face. It roared and rolled off before it disappeared.

"This isn't over yet." Xav climbed to his feet, hands raised. "Not even close."

I glanced toward Matt, who shrugged.

"Keep duelling."

Fuck.

14

I MADE a bubble and disappeared just as Xav did the same. I anticipated the move after I had used it. That would make this all the more challenging.

I took a shallow breath and stood completely still, eyes and ears open.

I thought I heard a shuffle. I heard my breath. There it was again. I grinned.

Xav was taller and heavier than me. Every step he took pressed the grass down under his shoes. He might as well have announced his presence. Lucky for me, the moon had done that for me.

Footprint, footprint, footprint. The grass bounced back behind him, but I watched his slow, careful process as he went. The shuffling stopped. He must have realised the sound was audible. As long as he didn't realise the grass betrayed his presence, I could use it to my advantage.

The question was, what did I do with this information? I chewed my lip and thought.

I couldn't blast him while he was in a bubble. His bubble could absorb my magic and give him the chance to throw it back at me. While possibly not deadly, it would knock me off my feet again, and make me vulnerable to whatever else he had up his sleeve.

I rubbed the new tattoo on my arm, carefully crafted beside the first one. No creature I created would get past his bubble, no matter how badass.

Unless…

I followed his steps with my eyes as he circled around to where I thought he might be. I pictured him waving his arm in front of him, but touching nothing. I almost felt his frustration. I smiled. Good, let him get angry and careless.

I stalked toward him on tiptoe, each step silent and light. When I got close enough, I turned to the side and stuck out my leg.

Xav stepped forward and tripped.

"What the fuck?" In his surprise, he dropped his bubble and appeared in front of me on his hands and knees. Shame I didn't have time for any snide remarks. A few good ones came to mind.

Before he could think to respond, I dropped my own bubble and slammed him the rest of the way to the ground with a fist of magic. He flailed his arms and legs, but I wasn't going to let him up, not until this was done.

"How long do I have to wait?" I asked over my shoulder.

"For the count of ten," Gunter replied.

I was glad he was the one who answered. It made Xav even more furious, and gave more legitimacy to my win.

Xav muttered something I couldn't make out. I pressed my magic down a little harder.

"What was that?" I cocked my head at him.

"Piss off," he growled.

"Charming." I smiled sweetly. "One. Two. Three…" I counted slowly.

"Four. Five." Matt moved to stand beside me, a grin on his face.

We counted together. "Six. Seven. Eight. Nine."

"Ten." Gunter said firmly. "Peyton wins. Let him up." Without another word, he turned and walked away.

I shrugged and lifted the magic from Xav's chest.

He jumped to his feet. For a moment I thought he might leap at me. Instead, he curled his lip and stalked back toward the UA building, Kylie on his heels.

"Nothing like a good loser," I said sarcastically. A moment later I was almost bowled over by Kane in his enthusiasm to hug me.

"I can't believe you actually won by tripping him." Kane laughed and kissed my lips. "I bet he didn't expect that."

I kissed him back, then leaned back to smile at him. "That was the general idea. Use your enemy's weakness against them. He was bigger, heavier and cockier."

"I don't know about cockier," Matt said.

I stuck my tongue out at him. "If I'm a handful, it's only because you're rubbing off on me."

"You wish," he murmured, but the look he gave me suggested he was the one doing the wishing.

I didn't know what to say to that. It wasn't as though I hadn't imagined us tearing each other's clothes off. Gods, just the thought made me wet.

"It's a little cold out here for that," Kane said, sounding regretful.

I blinked. It was? I felt kinda hot… Oh, I guess he was right, when I thought about it.

"Yeah, um, I guess we should go inside then." I glanced at Matt, but his face was turned away.

"Dyson will want to know you won," Kane said, seemingly oblivious to whatever this was between Matt and I.

"Yes he will," I agreed. Thinking about Dyson was a lot less complicated than thinking about Matt. Or Nash for that matter. If he found out what I had done, he'd be furious. Thank the gods I had won. Maybe now I wouldn't have to explain.

"WHAT THE HELLS WERE YOU THINKING?" Speak of the dragon… Nash stood beside the door which led into the UA, arms crossed over his chest. His gaze took me in, mouth set in a firm line, but eyes betraying the depths of his feelings for me. He was worried. More than that, he cared about me as more than a lover. I could have happily drowned in that look. What did I do to deserve the affection of any of these guys?

I gave Nash a smile. "I was thinking…it might be a nice night for a walk, sir."

He didn't buy it for a second, I saw that on his face as well. He glared at Kane and Matt. "Both of you as well. I should have you all tossed out on your asses."

"But you won't, will you, sir?" I stepped closer, put a hand on his chest and looked up at him. "I did win after all. Xav will leave us alone *and* he owes me a favour."

"You could have lost." Nash was still angry, but the edge came off his voice slightly.

"Then we would have dealt with it," I said firmly. I stopped and frowned. "How did you know anyway?"

Nash gave me a soft, but somewhat sheepish look. "I came looking for you. Imagine my annoyance when Ariana told me what you were up to."

"Oh." What was done, was done.

"I guess you better make it up to me," he said softly.

"No offence, sir, but Dyson will want to know Peyton won," Kane said.

"Then go and tell him." Nash didn't take his eyes off my face.

"But—" Kane sighed. "I don't think that's fair, sir, pulling rank. Maybe we should ask what Peyton wants."

Oh great, now I was under pressure. I glanced at Kane and frowned.

"Maybe I don't want to choose."

"Rock, paper, scissors." Kane held out his hand.

Nash arched an eyebrow at him. "Really? Are we in high school?"

"It feels like it sometimes, sir." I pointed out. "I mean, Xav acted like it."

"That doesn't mean we should." In spite of that, Nash stuck out his hand. Both guys shook their fists and revealed their choice.

"Paper beats rock, sir," Kane said, delighted.

Nash scowled, but stepped back. "Fine. I'll step aside gracefully. For now."

I shot him a smile as Kane laced his hand in mine. "Sorry, sir. Later."

He nodded. "Be glad there will be a later."

I grinned and turned away to see Matt still standing behind me. His expression was unreadable.

I let Kane's hand go and moved toward Matt.

"Thanks for all your help," I said softly. I leaned up to kiss him lightly on the mouth.

As least, that was my intention. One of us deepened the kiss, and before I knew it, we had dancing tongues, and breath coming in pants.

I don't know who pulled away first, but we snapped apart. Before I could say another word, Matt turned on his heel and was gone.

"Okay then," I said under my breath.

"Try not to let him bother you," Kane said. "He's confused."

"*He's* confused?" I asked. "He's not the only one. I don't know whether I'm coming or going with him." Although I was pretty sure I wasn't coming.

Kane slung an arm over my shoulder. "At least with me, you know where you stand. And in case you don't, I'm head over heels for you."

I gave him a soft smile. "You're a special guy and I care about you a lot." Was it love? It was pretty damned close. The only problem with love was, I'd have to make a choice. Wouldn't I? I still wasn't ready for that. I wasn't sure I would ever be. Life was complicated enough without having to break anyone's heart.

Kane gave me a soft kiss on the mouth and we walked together across the grass.

"You did amazing tonight, er, this morning," Kane said. "The tiger was cool, but using something as simple as tripping a guy..." He chuckled. "I wish more people were around to see it."

I grinned. "I bet Xav is glad there wasn't. Beaten by a girl, with the help of the oldest trick in the book."

"He was so sure he would win. He'll be licking

his wounds for a while." Kane opened the door leading into his room and gestured for me to go first.

"I hope so," I replied. "Where's Dyson?"

Kane frowned. "He should be here." He poked the top bunk with a few fingers, but no grunts of protest came in response. "It looks slept in."

"Maybe he went to the toilet?" I suggested.

"I guess so. Or he decided to give us some privacy." Kane stepped closer to me and wound his arms around me.

"That's possible, but we would have found somewhere else if he wanted us to."

Something about this didn't feel right. We had surmised that someone from the AMM had been working for Zeta. They could have snuck onto campus while Kane, Matt, and I were distracted and snatched Dyson from under our noses. If they still wanted him for their experiment then they could have—"

"Oh hey, guys." Dyson walked in through the door as though nothing was up. He tucked his phone into his back pocket. "How did things go?" He seemed distracted.

"Good. I turned Kane into a purple elephant and he stepped all over Xav," I replied.

"Great, great." Dyson nodded, then frowned. My words apparently sunk in. "Wait, what?"

I chuckled. "I won."

"Right, good. Of course you did." He kissed my cheek and pulled off his shirt. "Well, it's late and I need my beauty sleep."

I exchanged confused looks with Kane, who shrugged.

"We'll go somewhere else for a while then," Kane said awkwardly.

"Okay." Dyson stashed his phone under his pillow, slid out of his pants and climbed up onto his bunk.

"Are you feeling all right?" Kane asked him.

"Sure, just tired." Dyson rolled over so his back was to us and pulled the covers over himself.

"Oookay." Kane rubbed his forehead.

"Maybe we should do this another time," I suggested. Dyson was right about one thing, it was late. We'd have to be in class in a few hours.

"I'm sorry," Kane whispered.

I patted his shoulder and pressed a kiss to his mouth. "It's fine. It'll give me something to look forward to." As much as I enjoyed getting down and dirty with Kane, his place was here with his brother. "Let me know if either of you need anything."

I gave Dyson, or his back at least, a long look. He seemed to be asleep already, but I sensed he was at least partially aware I was still in the room. Had I done something to offend him? I hoped not. At least if I had, I'd like to think he could tell me, so I could fix it.

"I guess I'll see you both at breakfast." I flashed Kane a quick smile, then ducked out the door and closed it behind me. I stood in the corridor for a moment and listened. If the guys were talking, I couldn't hear it.

I realised I shouldn't be eavesdropping and hurried off toward my own room.

15

THE MOOD in the dining hall was strange. I felt it the moment I stepped inside. People stopped talking and looked in my direction. Of course they would; word of the duel would have spread faster than fire on a pile of dry leaves.

But... there was something else. When I looked back, no one would meet my gaze. Phones, which students had been looking at intently, suddenly clicked off.

I frowned at a couple of people, but their eyes were always lower than my face. Always on my...

I flushed. There was no way...

My heart racing, I grabbed some breakfast and hurried to slip into the chair beside Ariana.

"What the hells is going on?" I whispered.

She stared at me with wide eyes. "You haven't seen?"

"Seen what?" I searched her face, but my heart sank deeper and deeper.

"Check your phone," she said in a rough whisper.

I pulled mine out of my pocket and pressed on the screen. "Just a message from—" I peered closely, but didn't recognise the sender. "I have a feeling I shouldn't click on that." I wished it was something as benign as a virus which would wipe all my data before sending itself to all of my contacts and wiping all of theirs. Even a visit from fully armed Zeta agents might be preferable.

I swallowed and pressed on the message.

"What the fuck?" There, in living colour, was the photo Kane had taken of me. I had been halfway to thinking someone had filmed us and sent the video around to the whole school. Somehow, this was so much worse. This photo had been taken in a moment of intimacy, between two people who meant it to stay between them.

At least, that was what I had thought.

Tears prickled my eyes. "How could he have done this to me?" I closed the message and slammed my phone down on the table. How it didn't shatter, I don't know.

"Maybe it wasn't him?" Ariana suggested. She didn't seem even slightly convinced. Kane had taken the photo, how else would it have been sent to—as far as I could tell—the entire, fucking academy?

"I can't decide," I said between clenched teeth. "If I should kill him fast or slow." A little of both, perhaps. I had *trusted* him. Cared about him. What a bloody idiot I had been.

"I'm sure there's an explan—" I cut Ariana off when I leapt to my feet.

"I'm not hungry." I snatched my phone off the table and stomped toward the door.

Every step was followed by snickering and whispers. Didn't they understand? This wasn't some great joke. It wasn't just about me being humiliated. I had been violated, as sure as if I'd been held down and forced. My body, my trust…

Tears slid down my cheeks. I wanted to turn around and blast the entire room until every snide smile and nasty word was gone.

Instead, I swallowed and stepped outside into the autumn sunshine. The moment I felt concrete under my feet, I started to run.

I ran until the concrete gave way to grass. The stupid, fucking skirt flapped at my legs and the tie threatened to wind around my neck. I didn't stop until sweat trickled down my back and breathing became more difficult.

The pain settled into a dull ache in my chest, but I slowed to a walk.

"Peyton!"

Kane's voice was barely audible over the pounding of blood in my ears. That and I didn't want to see him, much less listen to anything he had to say.

"Peyton!" He was closer now.

I ignored him.

"Peyton, please stop and listen!"

I glanced over my shoulder. "Go away, Kane. There's nothing you can say to me I'd want to hear." I caught a look of hurt before I turned away.

"It wasn't me," he called out after me. "I swear on…on my entire collection of Godzilla comics."

I stopped and looked back again. "You have Godzilla comics?"

He shrugged. "We, they're graphic novels. Don't tell anyone I called them comics."

"Right now, I'm inclined to tell *everyone* you called them comics," I said dryly. "But I don't think anyone would care. They're more interested in staring at my tits."

He flushed. "I promised you I would never share that photo, and I didn't. Scout's honour."

"You were a Boy Scout?" I raised an eyebrow at him.

He smiled. "No. Geek's honour then. That's unbreakable." He raised a hand with his fingers spread apart, Vulcan style.

I sighed. I was half way to believing him, but I felt as if that photo had ripped a piece of my heart out. The thing was, I *wanted* to believe him. Not just because I didn't want to think my judgment was so flawed, but because I cared about him. The very idea that someone would stab me in the heart…

I swallowed down a new round of tears. "If you didn't, then who did?"

Kane licked his lips. "I don't know," he said tentatively.

I frowned. My mind conjured up a very unwelcome image of Dyson and his strange behaviour last night.

I shook my head. "You can't possibly think…"

"I don't know," Kane said quickly. "But he was acting weird. This morning, too. He barely looked at me. I tried to talk to him, but he hardly said a thing before he went off to breakfast. He didn't even wait."

My legs gave out. I plopped down on the grass. "I

didn't see him at breakfast." Surely I would have noticed him amongst the other students? He certainly hadn't been at the table with Ariana.

"I don't understand why he'd do something like this. Unless…"

Kane sat beside me and put a hand on my knee. "Unless what?" he asked gently.

I shook my head. "Is there any chance Zeta got to him in some way?"

"Why would Zeta want photos of you spread around?" Kane asked.

I shrugged. "To humiliate me?" Yeah, that sounded bizarre to me too. "Maybe they wanted to drive a wedge between us. This would be one way to do it."

"I suppose so." He gave my knee a squeeze. "You do believe me though, don't you? I would never do something like this. Not to *anyone*, but especially not to you. You're not like anyone I've ever met. I wouldn't hurt you, not for anything."

"What if you had to do something to me, in order to save Dyson?" I asked. It wasn't a fair question, but he had to mull over the possibility. The gods only knew what Zeta might try to push us into.

Kane hesitated. "I don't know," he admitted. "I'll

do whatever I can to make sure it never comes to that. We can't let them beat us."

"And what about Dyson?" I asked. "If he's working with them…"

Kane looked stricken. "I can't believe he would. There must be some sort of logical explanation for all of this."

"Such as?"

"He could have been sleep walking?"

"Has he ever done that before?" I cocked my head at him.

"No," Kane admitted. "There's a first time for everything though, right?"

I exhaled softly. "I suppose it's possible, but that wouldn't explain why he wouldn't talk to you this morning."

Kane rubbed his chin. He had just enough stubble there to be a little rough, but I liked it. He looked sexy.

"I'm sure it was something which isn't a big deal," he said slowly.

I looked down at the grass, then back up again. "Is it possible he's seeing someone else?" He had told me he wanted to take things slowly with me, but that could be because another person was in the picture.

"No," Kane said so quickly I flinched. "He cares

about you as much as I do. He told me so yesterday. Or was it the day before?" He frowned. "Either way, if there was someone he would have told you. And me."

"So, why the photo?" I lay back on the grass and looked up at the blue sky. A cloud scudded above me, wisps of white like lace trailing out behind it.

"We still don't know it was him." Kane lay down beside me and snuck a hand up my skirt. "We should try to talk to him."

"Right, we should," I agreed. "Before we get side-tracked." This was a bit too public for my taste, especially after the morning I'd had.

"I'm sorry." He stroked inside my thigh. "I kinda wish I hadn't taken that photo. Then none of this would have happened."

"If it hadn't been that, it would have been something else."

"I guess so." He snuck a finger under the side of my panties.

I covered my hand with his. "I can't, not out here."

He stopped, then drew out his hand. "I understand. Whoever sent that photo really did a number on you, didn't they?"

I sighed. "Yeah, they really did. Fuckers."

Kane chuckled. "That's my Peyton. Nothing holds you back for long."

I smiled. Part of me wanted to strip and screw him silly, right there in the middle of the running field. To hells with idiots like Xav, or whoever had circulated that photo. Another part of me wanted to pack my belongings and go home to my parents. I try to be badass, but a girl can only take so much humiliation.

"Let's go and find Dyson and get this cleared up." I stood and offered Kane my hand. "Then we can figure out who really sent that photo around."

"Atta girl," Kane rose and squeezed my hand. "I'm sure it'll all be a big misunderstanding."

"Yeah."

But I doubted it. Whoever had sent that message was trying to make my life hells, I was certain of that. If this didn't work, they'd try something else. Then there was the problem of Dyson. Photo or no photo, he was acting cagey as fuck. I thought I knew him well enough to know he didn't act like that without a good reason. The problem was, I wasn't sure I really knew him at all.

"Where would he be right now?" I asked.

"Hmmm. If he's finished breakfast, he's probably in one of the computer labs, studying."

One thing I had to give UA credit for, they had the best computers of any school I had attended. Every centimetre was the latest of everything, and they had granted the AMM students full access to all of it. Oh sure, some of their students bitched, but we ignored them. It wasn't as though we had anywhere else to go to use them. Even if we have computers as good as theirs, our rooms were too small to work in comfort.

"Okay, let's go and see." I took Kane's hand and ignored the looks we got when we approached the school and stepped back into the corridors.

Someone whistled, but I suppressed the urge to send my gargoyle or tiger after them. That would be the perfect way to get thrown out and I might regret the damage my creature caused.

Maybe.

Kane sighed. "I'm really, really sorry. If I'd known…"

I shook my head. "It's not your fault some people are assholes." I hesitated for a moment before I added, "Do you really have a Godzilla comic collection?"

"Graphic novels, but yes." He nodded. "Do you want to read them some time?"

"Sure, why not? My geek card might lapse if I don't take it out for a spin once in a while."

He grinned. "Great. Can I teach you the Vulcan salute?"

I laughed and gave him one. "I nailed that long ago," I said proudly.

"Geeks unite."

We laughed, but the sound was strained. It probably would be until we got everything straightened out.

If we did.

"HEY, DYS." Kane sounded cheerful, but with an undertone of anxiety in his voice.

Dyson glanced up and smiled. "Hey." His gaze lingered on me, laced with warmth. "What's up? You two look as though you lost that duel last night."

Kane and I exchanged confused looks. His brother seemed to be his usual, jovial self, with no hint of the distance he'd shown earlier.

"Are you feeling okay?" Kane asked him.

"Of course," Dyson replied. "Are you?" He closed the computer in front of him, but I hadn't seen anything on the screen but classwork.

"Did you see the photo someone spread around the school?" I asked. I watched his expression carefully.

Dyson sighed and looked regretful. "I did. I'm sorry about that. Are you okay?"

"You're sorry?" Kane echoed.

Dyson frowned. He picked up a pencil and toyed with the end of it. "Of course. As in, I'm sorry someone was such a dick to you. Who was it?"

I considered for a moment, then pulled over a chair and sat beside him. "We don't know. We hoped you might have some idea."

Dyson tapped the pencil against his lip. "Ideas, sure. Evidence? Nope, none. I would suggest their enrolment form says University of Arcana, rather than Academy of Modern Magic. After what we all went through last year, none of us would attack you. Except…"

"Yes?" I prompted.

"Whoever told Zeta where to find us." Dyson shrugged and placed the pencil down on the table beside the computer.

I shook my head. "I hate to say it, but I think this is old-fashioned schoolyard bullying. Well, the modern version of it. Xav is probably pissed I beat him. The fact he or his friends would hack Kane's phone to get back at me is pretty fucking childish, if you ask me."

"It is," Dyson agreed.

"Why were you acting weird last night?" Kane blurted.

Dyson cocked his head at his brother. "What are you talking about?" He seemed genuinely confused. He looked at me, then back at Kane.

"After the duel, you seemed uninterested. Then again this morning, you barely said a word." Kane leaned against the wall and crossed his arms. "It's not like you. I usually can't shut you up."

Dyson frowned. "I don't even remember seeing you after the duel. I didn't know about it until…" He scratched his head. "I don't know."

"Are you stoned?" Kane asked bluntly.

"Fuck no." Dyson looked horrified at the idea. "You know me, I prefer to be high on life, not illicit substances. Besides, drugs and dogs don't mix."

"That sounds like a bumper sticker," I remarked.

"It does, doesn't it?" Dyson agreed. "Or a t-shirt."

"Or—"

Kane cut me off. "Can we focus, please?" He paused for a moment before he added, "Owls and opiates don't mix sounds better."

Dyson leaned over in his chair to sock Kane on the arm.

"So anyway," I sat back in the chair. "What's the last thing you clearly remember?"

"Um." Dyson rubbed his chin. "I remember having dinner. You looked extra cute with your hair in a ponytail."

I flushed but waved for him to go on.

"I was watching you eat spaghetti and thinking about your mouth. The way you slurp those noodles." He fanned himself with his hand.

"Right?" Kane said. "I've never seen anyone look so hot while eating pasta."

"You guys will give me a big head," I told them.

Dyson pointed to his lap. "It's too late for me."

My gaze ventured lower, to the front of his pants. "So I see. We should probably focus, though."

Both guys sighed simultaneously.

"You're right," Dyson said. "After dinner I came here and got some work done on an essay. After that —" He frowned. "It's foggy."

Kane and I shared a look of concern.

"Is mind control magic a thing?" Kane asked.

"Not that I'm aware of," I replied. "What about shifters? Is there some way to influence your actions?" Kane was studying paranormal science. If anyone would know, it was him.

Kane shook his head slowly. "Just the usual substances normals are susceptible to: alcohol, narcotics, sugar."

"Kids and sugar is universal," Dyson remarked. "But the only sugar I've had all week was a donut."

I immediately started to crave one of the sweet treats. AMM would have had them on the menu, but no such luck here.

"How did you get a donut?" Kane asked. "I don't remember you leaving campus for a sugar hit."

Dyson frowned. "One of the women in my history class had some. She was handing them out. She even brought in a pink one for me, because she knew I can't eat chocolate."

I frowned. "Who is this woman?"

"Jealous?" Kane asked.

"Suspicious," I said firmly, "of her."

"She's new to the academy," Dyson supplied. "She transferred from somewhere…" He shook his head. "I don't remember."

"Funny that," I said sarcastically. "Just a wild guess here, but she's left already."

Kane frowned. "That's not nearly as important as why she was here. If Zeta has found a way to control shifters…"

My blood ran cold. "You're right. That would mean they know we're here. Instead of attacking with a full-scale assault, they're testing to see what they might do to us."

Dyson shuddered. "Drugging me so I'll send a naked photo of Peyton to everyone seems a strange thing to do though."

I shook my head. "I don't think those things are related. The photo was just some asshole thinking they could get to me. The drugging…that's something else entirely." It was a bizarre coincidence, but I was sure that was all it was.

"It wasn't a very good attempt," Kane said.

"No. Drugging someone against their will usually isn't," I agreed.

"No, I mean—" Kane looked thoughtful. "We knew something happened. He was acting stranger than usual."

Dyson gave him a lopsided smile. "Thanks for noticing. I think."

"You're welcome." Kane flashed him a smile. "The question is, is it still in your bloodstream, and what is it? Do you feel different or odd in any way?"

Dyson's brow creased in concentration. "No more than usual."

"Can you shift?" I asked.

"Is that related in some way, or do you want to see me naked?" Dyson grinned. "I'm happy to oblige any time."

"We know you are," Kane groaned. He covered

his eyes with his hands and rubbed his forehead. "I guess it's a relevant question. Go ahead and try."

"Thanks for permission, bro." Dyson stood and pulled his shirt off over his head.

"Yeah. You're welcome, bro." Kane slumped into a chair and turned away.

For someone who liked having sex in public, he really didn't like seeing his brother naked. Maybe it was all about context. Like how I didn't mind people seeing me having sex, but I didn't want nude photos shared around. If I had done the sharing, I might be okay with it.

Unlike Kane, I didn't look away while Dyson stripped. His body was firm and perfectly toned. I wanted to pour chocolate sauce over his abs and lick it off slowly.

I might have licked my lips.

Dyson saw and grinned. For as long as I had known him, he had never been shy about strutting around naked in front of people. Far from it. I would bet he was the kind of kid who pulled his clothes off as soon as he was old enough to do it by himself.

It was just another part of his charm.

"Okay, let's see." He folded his pants and tossed them onto a chair along with his underpants. He gave me a wink when he noticed my eyes on his dick.

I shrugged. What can I say, I liked his dick.

Smiling, Dyson lowered his face and stood still.

His smile faded, brow creased.

He closed his eyes and bared his teeth. "What. The. Fuck."

Eyes wide, he stared at Kane.

Kane jerked to his feet, his face pale. "You can't shift?"

I gaped at him. Oh gods, what had Zeta done to him. If they…

"I—" Dyson shifted into his big, shaggy dog form. He bared his teeth and huffed out a breath which sounded like he was laughing.

"Fucker," Kane muttered.

"For once, I might agree with you," I told him. I willed my heart to slow from its painful pounding. "That was a mean trick." I had been half way to assuming Zeta had discovered a way to prevent shifters from…well, being shifters. The idea made me shudder.

"He should definitely be in the doghouse for that one." Kane flopped back into his chair so quickly it almost rolled out from under him.

Dyson shifted back. "Sorry, I couldn't resist."

I gave him a dark look from behind my eyebrows. "Try harder next time." I wasn't really that angry with him, but I probably should be. He had scared the living daylights out of Kane and I.

"I guess that answers that question," Dyson said, his expression apologetic at least. "Unless the pink donut wore off already."

"If there's anything I know about donuts, it's that they don't just wear off," I said dryly. "They have to be worked off."

Dyson chuckled, but Kane still looked as if he might be sick all over the floor.

"I need some air." Kane stood on unsteady legs.

"We'll go with you." I offered him my hand.

He waved it away. "It's okay, I need a few moments alone. Then we're going to the lab to take some blood from Dyson. If you're lucky, I'll leave a little."

"My blood seems to be busy." Dyson looked downward.

"Put your pants on and keep it in there," Kane said. "Peyton is right, you might work off the donut. If we can find even a trace of whatever it was, it'll help."

Dyson pulled a face, but picked up his underpants. "You're the science geek."

"That's right." Kane nodded. "Get dressed and I'll meet you in the lab."

"Yes, sir." Dyson gave him a sarcastic salute.

Kane sighed and muttered something about Dyson being his usual self before he hurried out the door.

"Was I really that different?" Dyson asked. He leaned against the wall while he pulled his underpants on.

"You were…distant," I replied. "It felt as though you weren't all there. Like—maybe you had a lot on your mind."

"Well," he said lightly, "we all know that's not true. It's me we're talking about."

"Hey." I gave him my best stern-possible-future-teacher face. "You can be deep when you want to be."

"Except right now." He pouted.

"What happened to taking things slowly?" I asked.

He shrugged with one shoulder. "That was BPD. Before Pink Donut," he added when I gave him a questioning look. "If Zeta can really get to me here, then life might be too short."

I swallowed back a ball of emotion which threatened to leave me choked up. "Don't say things like that." He was right though. If we weren't safe here, and apparently we weren't, then we could expect Zeta to attack at any moment.

He pulled on his uniform pants, which hugged his ass like a glove and took my hand.

"Fine, how about I talk like this," he said softly. "I'm falling for you. Every day I feel more and more, until I don't know why it doesn't swallow me. I wanted to take it slowly because I didn't want to screw this up. You're more than a fling. You're someone I could see myself being with for a long, long time. Even if I have to share you with Kane and whoever else is in your life."

I wiped a tear from my cheek. "I care about you, too. If anything happened to you…" I sniffed.

"It won't," he assured me.

If only I felt so confident.

17

THE LAB WAS COLD. That wasn't surprising, most of the UA was, especially the places the AMM students used. Maybe I shouldn't be so paranoid, the UA students looked just as cold as the rest of us. They sat around the tables and workbenches, huddled in their jackets. Some of them even wore scarves. Unlike the rest of their clothes, the scarves apparently didn't need to be a regulation colour or length. One woman wore a bright pink one, while another looked like a House from Harry Potter.

"Figures she'd be a Slytherin," Dyson muttered.

I grinned. "Yeah, hashtag not shocked."

In spite of that, I gave the group a smile. They nodded in return. Perhaps not friendly, but not outright hostile, either. One or two even gave me glances which suggested they were impressed. They weren't even looking at my breasts, so I guessed it was about the duel, not the photo. Thank the gods. If they wanted to talk about me, I preferred that topic.

"Science geeks," Dyson said under his breath.

"Are you geek shaming?" I asked, one eyebrow arched at him.

"Not all all," he said breezily. "I love geeks. I am one too."

"Sure." I drew the word out. "I hope you're not science shaming then, because I happen to think science is cool."

He held up both hands in surrender. "You're right, it is, but people who study it are a whole other level of geeky. Take Kane for instance. He's bordering on being a nerd."

"Is there a difference?" I sat on a stool, my back to a workbench.

"It's subtle, but it exists." Dyson nodded. "Geeks are the cool version of nerds."

"Okay, thanks for clarifying that." I gave him a funny look, but grinned.

"Anytime." He placed his hands on the bench, one to either side of me. He leaned in until we were nose to nose. His breath brushed my cheek.

"I'd hate for you to think I was working for the

enemy," he said softly. "I'd hate to *be* working for the enemy and not realise it."

I put a hand lightly on his cheek. "I would hate that, too, but we'll get to the bottom of this." I wasn't sure we shouldn't run like hells if there was any chance Zeta knew we were here, but we needed the information this lab could give us. As labs went, it was the only one we had any access to. For all we knew, Dyson had really just sleep walked, and all the worry was for nothing. Deep down, I suspected there was much more to this than that. I hated the idea they might have gotten to Dyson, not just for my sake, but for everyone's, especially his. Who knew what they might do to him, or with him?

I swallowed down a knot of emotion which built up in my throat.

"Yeah." He pressed a kiss to my lips, then stepped away, his expression unreadable.

Of all the guys, Dyson was the one I had always struggled to understand. At times he seemed so laid back and open, but much of the time I couldn't guess what was going on in his head. If I was honest with myself, I might admit it scared me a little. If he was working with Zeta and planned to betray us all, I wouldn't know until it was too late. I doubted even Kane would know.

My stomach turned at the idea.

"Are you all right?" Dyson asked. Evidently I was easier to read.

"I'm fine." I was mostly not lying.

"Great. Here comes Kane." Dyson nodded toward the door.

"Roll up your sleeve," Kane told him.

Dyson supported his elbow with his opposite hand and cupped his chin. "Are you qualified to take my blood?"

"No, now roll up your sleeve." Kane grabbed a needle and a vial and nodded toward his brother.

"See what I mean about science geeks?" Dyson said cheerfully. He pulled his sleeve up to his bicep and held out his arm.

I smiled. "Yeah, but he's helping you, so down boy."

"Yes ma'am." He gave me a sly smile.

I responded by sticking out my tongue.

"I can think of better uses for that," Dyson said.

I wiggled my tongue, then drew it back to say, "I'll bet you can. That will have to wait." I caught Kane glancing over to the other students. His Adam's apple bobbed up and down. With him, I knew just what he was thinking, and he'd do it, too. Right there on the workbench. I wondered what the other students would think or do.

I sighed. I wouldn't dare to try to find out. There was enough tension between the UA students and me as it was, without alienating ones who seemed more tolerant.

Kane sighed a moment later. I suspect he'd come to the same conclusion I had. He shook his head slightly and jabbed the needle into Dyson's vein.

Dyson winced. "Ouch, dude."

"Sorry." Kane filled the vial with blood, then drew out the needle and handed me a bandage to put on Dyson's puncture wound. "Don't shift until you stop bleeding."

"Where did you learn to take blood?" I asked while he capped the vial and took it off to a corner full of equipment.

"I watch TV," Kane said. He smiled faintly. "Our mother is a nurse. She wanted me to be a doctor, so she taught me a few things. If I'm going to study paranormal physiology, it's something I'll need to do."

"He used to practice on me," Dyson remarked.

"Only with syringes without needles," Kane said. "The needles were reserved for our teddy bears."

"Mine you mean," Dyson said. "He would never practice on Mr Snuggles."

I grinned. "You have a bear called Mr Snuggles?"

Kane blushed bright red. "I was three when I named him. Anyway, Dyson's was called Miss Pussy. He couldn't tell a bear from a cat."

I smothered a laugh. "I suppose they could look a bit alike."

"For your information," Dyson declared, loud and firm, "nothing else looks like a pussy. I was young and naive at the time. That's my excuse and I'm sticking to it." He crossed his arms over his chest and nodded.

I patted his shoulder. "I believe you."

"This might take a while," Kane said. "Maybe you two can go and study, or…whatever."

"I like whatevering," Dyson said. He glanced toward me.

"I'm fond of it myself," I agreed. "I could whatever all day."

"Me too." Dyson grinned. He held out his hand. "Come on, let's leave Captain Science Geek to solve the mysteries of the universe."

I took Dyson's hand and gave Kane a kiss on the cheek. He responded with a distracted smile. I guessed he was in his element here and we should leave him to it. I would have liked to help, or at least watch, but I really had no idea what I was looking at. Besides, we'd probably distract him and slow him down anyway.

"Oh," Kane said before we'd taken more than two steps. "Be careful and don't take cake from strangers." He shot Dyson a frown that seemed laced with further meaning. He trusted his twin implicitly, but was worried about what influence he might be under.

"I'm fine, I swear," Dyson assured him. "I feel like my normal, paranormal self. I haven't done anything strange for at least a few minutes." He smiled sweetly and batted his eyelashes.

Kane took a moment before nodding. "Fine, but still be careful. If they tried anything once, they might well try again."

"We will be," I said firmly. "We'll be all about being careful and trusting no one." Even each other. That sucked, because I really, really wanted to be alone with Dyson. Naked. And sweaty. "Although, we should fill Nash in on what happened."

"And Matt," Kane said.

I grimaced. "Him too, I guess." I nodded and headed out of the lab and into warmer air.

"Nash is probably teaching right now," Dyson remarked.

"Right. And Matt is probably in class. What is he studying anyway?"

Dyson frowned. "Would you believe, I have no idea? Knowing him it's something to do with killing Zeta agents."

"Is there a degree for that?"

"Bachelor of Death and Destruction to Assholes?" Dyson suggested. "I'm not even sure what faculty that would come under."

I shrugged with one shoulder. "I suspect it comes under humanities."

"Right," Dyson drew the word out. "He could double major in death and destruction and minor in something fun, like theatre."

"That sounds accurate." I nodded and tried to hold back a smile. "I can imagine him up on stage, makeup and all." Honestly I couldn't imagine anything more unlikely, but the idea cheered me up a little.

"What sounds accurate?"

Matt spoke so suddenly behind me, I jumped and whirled around.

"Speak of the devil," Dyson drawled. "We were just discussing what you might be studying."

"Ah." Matt didn't seem interested in elaborating, so we drew him to the side of the corridor and told him everything that had happened after the duel, up until now. He eyed Dyson with the mistrust he gave to pretty much everyone anyway.

"Should we be packing?" The gods knew why I always deferred to Matt. He seemed to have connections to the Paranormal Council, but when it came down to it, he was a second year, like me. One whose ass I had saved in the Zeta attack on the AMM.

Matt rubbed his forehead. "I'll look into it. In the meantime, just keep doing what you normally do. It's possible they don't know we're onto them yet. If we start acting strangely... More than usual, they'll realise."

"If there's anyone watching," I said.

Matt's brow creased. Damn, why was he so adorable when he did that?

"There's little doubt someone is watching," he said slowly, but firmly. "They could be anyone, anywhere." He gave Dyson a meaningful look.

Dyson bristled. "I'm not working for them."

"I didn't say you were," Matt replied coolly, "but you'd say that if you weren't."

Dyson stepped toward him, hands in fists.

I gripped his hand to hold him back. "Don't. Fighting amongst ourselves is what they want."

"How do you know what they want?" Dyson dropped my hand.

I stared. "I beg your pardon? Did you just suggest *I* might be working with them?"

"No," he said hastily. "Of course not, but it would explain a few things."

"Like what?" I demanded.

He looked toward the floor. "Like how they always know where to find us."

"You working with them would also explain that," I pointed out coldly. "Remember the whole "Dyson acting weird" thing?"

His head jerked back up, eyes wide. "I already said—"

I cut him off. "I know what you said. You think I'm the one who is betraying us."

"I don't, I just—" Dyson glanced toward Matt, who raised his hands to indicate he was staying well out of this conversation.

"Someone is doing it," Dyson said finally.

"Well it's not me." I crossed my arms and stepped away from them both. Tears prickled in my eyes.

"But you're okay with thinking it might be me,"

Dyson said bitterly. "Don't deny it, I've seen it on your face since you stepped into the computer lab."

"I—" I couldn't deny it, and I loathed myself for it. "At least Kane is trying to find out what's going on."

"Yeah, he is. He'll prove I did nothing wrong."

"I'm sure he will," I said. I wasn't that sure and I knew it showed on my face.

Hurt filled Dyson's eyes before he turned and stalked away.

"Fuck," I muttered. If division was what Zeta wanted, they certainly had it. Dyson would probably never talk to me again.

My heart ached. I wanted to curl up in a ball and cry.

18

Matt shrugged. "Is there any point in telling you not to let him get to you?"

I gave him a sour look. "None." I sagged against the wall and bit back tears. "Is there really any chance he's involved?"

"There's a chance any of us could be," he replied. "Except me. I know I'm not."

I opened my mouth to make some kind of smart ass comment, but sighed instead. Having been offended only a couple of minutes earlier, I could hardly go around throwing stones at Matt. Besides, after all I had seen him do, I was ninety-nine percent certain he was on our side. It would be a hundred percent, but he didn't tell me everything about Zeta and the Paranormal Council and I suspected he withheld things I should know.

"I know you know I can be trusted," I said finally. He and Ariana had been asked to protect me after all.

"When it comes to Zeta, yes," he agreed. "Not with other things." A smile played around the corners of his mouth, so I knew he was teasing.

I wasn't much in the mood for it though. I grunted and started off down the corridor.

"Where are you going?" His long stride caught up with me quickly.

"I don't know, just walking."

"Do you want some company?"

"Not especially." This whole day sucked, winning the duel notwithstanding. To be honest, I couldn't care less about the stupid duel right now. Everything since then went to crap.

"If it's any consolation, the photo was very tasteful."

I stopped so suddenly the students walking behind us almost ran into the back of me. I expected them to give me a dirty look, but they wove around us without so much as a glance back.

"Tasteful?" I echoed.

"Sure. You know, more like art than porn." Matt's

expression was completely unapologetic. He actually seemed impressed.

I gaped at him for a moment, then kept walking. "I suppose it was. Do you know who hacked Kane's phone to send it to everyone?"

"No, but it's easy enough to find out."

I almost stopped again. "It is?"

"Yeah. Well, it'll be harder here than at the AMM, but it was probably a magical hack. The academy keeps a record of spells used on campus."

"Uhhh, like making tigers appear so they can attack other students?" Shit. How much trouble would I be in if they looked up *those* records?

"Making the tiger, yes, but not the why," Matt replied. "But don't worry, I have that covered. Or rather, Nash does. If anyone asks, he'll say you were training under his supervision."

I frowned. "He shouldn't have to lie for me."

"It won't be the first time, or the last," Matt said easily. "But it goes both ways. It probably already has."

"I guess so," I agreed uneasily. He was right though. I would lie for any of my friends or lovers, as long as no one was hurt as a result.

"Come on, let's find ourselves a hacker."

To my surprise, he grabbed my hand and tugged

me toward the basement the AMM admin had been relegated to. A bigger shock was the intensity of the jolt of heat his touch sent to my core. I felt as though he had ignited an inferno I hadn't known existed. One I suddenly, desperately, wanted to burn with him.

He gave me a look which suggested he felt it too, and dropped my hand.

"Sorry," he muttered.

"No you're not," I replied. "You're just sorry you like me more than you want to."

He looked over at me before we stepped into the basement. "Interesting theory. Liking you would be a conflict of interest. And probably a bad idea."

"That doesn't stop," I mouthed, "Nash."

"He makes his own choices," Matt replied. "I never said I thought they were good ones." He stepped inside and plonked himself down in front of a computer. None of the staff so much as gave him a second look.

"You'll have to explain that to me someday." I wheeled a chair over and sat beside him.

He glanced over his shoulder. "Yeah, someday." He turned on the screen and tapped in a password. "This is my personal account, so don't think I know the AMM's password."

"That thought hadn't crossed my mind." I had memorised his, though. I never knew when I might need to get access. "How many people would know spell logs are kept?"

He tapped on the keyboard. "It's not a secret, but they don't go around announcing it either."

I crossed my legs. "How does someone hack a phone?"

"With another phone," Matt replied without looking away from the screen.

"The UA doesn't use phones to do magic," I pointed out.

"No they don't," he agreed.

I blinked a couple of times. "But that would mean…"

Matt sat back and regarded me. "Don't assume you can trust everyone, just because they're AMM students."

"I wouldn't," I said quickly. "I didn't, I just…"

"Prefer to assume a UA student did it?" He turned back to the screen.

"Yes, I suppose. Dyson *did* say the pink donut woman was one of us."

"Trust no one," Matt said simply.

"Except you."

"Except me," he agreed.

"Trust the one person who doesn't like me."

"At least I'm impartial."

"Great." I snorted.

"You can trust Ariana and Nash," Matt added. "They like you, for some reason."

I would have stuck out my tongue at him, but his attention was all on the screen. Instead, I made a rude noise with my tongue.

He smiled and clicked the "return" key. "Okay, this should give us some idea. Although, I'm not sure if you're mature enough to deal with whatever we find."

Asshole.

"I'm plenty mature enough, so there."

"Mmmhmm, sure," he replied. The reflection of the screen showed in his eyes, words flickered upward rapidly.

"I had no idea so much magic was done here." I probably should have realised, but I had never given it any thought.

Matt looked as though he might say something, but his gaze snapped toward the screen. He pointed to a line of text.

"There, someone did a hacking spell at one am."

I peered where he pointed. "How can you tell?"

"It's a phone to phone transfer. If it was done voluntarily it wouldn't have needed magic."

"So…you're guessing?"

"Yes, but's an educated guess." He lowered his hand and scrolled down a few more lines. "There's nothing else here like it. Here's your tiger conjuring. There's Xav's two magical creatures." He leaned in closer and squinted. "That's odd."

"What?" I looked too, but I didn't know what I was looking at. "Is your major magical computer science, by any chance?"

He glanced at me. "Yeah. I worked on the development of this program."

"Oh." That made sense, and explained why he was trusted to use it. He was probably here all the time, updating it. "So what's odd?"

"Someone cast a protection spell. Like the magic bubbles we use."

"I know what a protection spell is," I said impatiently. "Why is that odd? I used one and so did Xav, remember?"

"Yes, but no one else there did."

I rubbed my forehead. "Are you saying someone else was out there, watching?"

"Exactly. Someone who didn't want us to know they were there."

"Can you tell who it was?"

Matt shook his head slowly. "No. It might have been a random passerby, who thought they'd stick around to watch. Or…"

"Someone who meant me harm?" I finished for him.

"It was probably someone who wanted to keep you safe." Matt exhaled loudly.

"That's not a bad thing, is it?" I asked.

"Only if they helped you in some way. Then you'll have to forfeit. Xav will have won the bet."

"No one helped me," I said insistently. "You were there, you saw the whole thing."

"I didn't see you when you were invisible," Matt pointed out.

I frowned. "I didn't have any help," I said again.

"Can you prove it?" he asked.

"Ye—no, I suppose not. Xav can't prove I did, though. They might have been there to help him."

Matt snorted a laugh. "If they did, they didn't do a very good job. But if anyone knows about this, they could insist you won by cheating."

I growled. "Please tell me we'll leave high school behind at some point."

"I've heard it lasts until you're forty and give away your last fuck," Matt said.

I grimaced. "Figures. Can you delete the record of whoever it was?"

He frowned. "I can, but I'm not sure I should."

"Do you want me to be accused of cheating?" I asked.

He hesitated.

I glared.

"Fine, but you owe me one."

"One what?" I said with thinking.

His Adam's apple bobbed. "I'll think of something."

Did I imagine the catch in his voice?

He deleted the line of text and updated the program. "There, your tracks are covered."

"Not *my* tracks," I commented. "So what about the phone hack? Can you see who did it?"

"That one is a little easier," he said. "Phones have numbers."

"No shit," I replied dryly. "So what?"

"So, just like calls are logged, so is magical use. Here is the number of the phone the photo was taken from." He pointed to the screen.

"That's Kane's number," I said after I checked it with my phone. "Whose is the other one?"

Matt grabbed a piece of paper and a pen and scribbled down the number. Or rather, wrote it quickly, but in neat, precise writing. "I don't know off the top of my head."

"Of course you don't. Who knows anyone's number from memory these days?" I gave him a look of disbelief. I quickly followed that with a snort. "Let me guess, you even remember your own number?"

"Of course I do, you don't?" He arched an eyebrow at me.

"I don't call myself, " I reasoned, "so, no."

He looked as though he might say something, but closed his mouth and shook his head instead.

"So…I already know it's not my number," he said slowly. "Because I would know it by looking, and I'm not a hacker. At least, not in regard to this matter." He smiled slyly.

"I think I'll file that under "things you probably shouldn't say in a university administration area." Unless you want to get arrested?"

He grinned. Damn him, he was too cute for his own good. Or mine.

"Not especially. I'm not into being restrained." He peered down the piece of paper and luckily missed my blush.

"Have you tried it?" I asked in spite of myself.

I knew I had said the wrong thing when a haunted look crossed his eyes.

"That's a whole other story I won't get into," he muttered. "Cross check the numbers on your phone and see if it matches anyone." He pushed the paper across the top of the table toward me.

"Okay." I opened my contacts and scrolled with one eye on the screen the other on the page.

"It's not Dyson's," I noted with some relief. "Or Ariana's." I hadn't considered her for a moment. "Not Hamish either. Or Nash. It's obviously neither of my parents', or..." I checked my phone, the paper and back again.

"This makes no sense."

"What? Whose is it?" Matt leaned over and squinted at my screen. "Why does that name seem familiar?"

I shook my head in confusion. "Jess is my best friend outside the academy. It couldn't have been her, she can't use a drop of magic."

"Just because she can't, doesn't mean it wasn't her phone," Matt said softly.

"But how—" My heart sank. "This wasn't bullying, was it? They're using her to get to me."

19

MATT PUT a hand on my shoulder before I leapt to my feet and ran out the door.

"What are you doing?" he hissed. "Apart from jumping to conclusions."

"They have her." I jerked away from him.

"They have her *phone*," he corrected. "Or had it at one in the morning. Apart from that, we know nothing."

"We know someone is trying to screw with me," I said bitterly. I sagged back in the chair and rubbed my face.

"We might know that," he conceded. "Going off half-cocked isn't going to help. We need more information."

"So we can go off full-cocked?" I suggested.

"Exactly." He smiled faintly. "When did you hear from her last? Or better yet, see her?"

"During the holiday. I...I've been busy." Yeah, okay, I sucked as a best friend. For all I know, she had been kidnapped by Zeta and I hadn't known.

Matt shrugged. "It happens. You haven't texted her or received a text from her?"

"No." I double-checked my phone just in case. The last text we'd shared was weeks ago.

"Social media?" Matt sat back and curled his hands around the arms of his chair.

I opened an app and clicked on her profile. "She posted two nights ago. She was off to some party with a group from Melbourne University." The post included a selfie of Jess with a big smile on her face, black hair, and a yellow t-shirt.

A wave of sadness washed over me. Even if she was fine, I missed her and the parties we used to go to together. We had been inseparable before I started at AMM.

I liked the post and closed the app.

"There's nothing after that." I tapped my fingers on the table. "Maybe I should shoot her off a text. It might—"

My phone beeped with the text tone. I frowned at the name of the sender.

"It's Jess." That couldn't be a coincidence. I had just liked her post. That might have alerted her, or whoever had her phone, that I was looking for her.

"Open it," Matt said.

I sucked in a breath and clicked on my messages. "Shit."

"What?"

I turned the screen so Matt could see the photo of Jess. She stared at the camera with wide eyes, full of fear. She wore the same yellow shirt she had on in her selfie, but her hair was a mess and her face was pale.

"Fuck," Matt muttered. "Any idea where she is?"

I looked back at the photo and searched behind her. She seemed to be on a stool in front of a table, or a bench of some kind. The detail was blurry, as if the sender didn't want me to see too much.

After a while, I shook my head. "It's nowhere I recognise. Maybe I should ask."

I thought Matt might laugh, but he looked thoughtful and nodded. "Yes, but not yet. We can call them, but we should have Nash in the room as well. He'll know what to listen for."

I nodded. I would feel better with Nash involved. Who was I kidding; he'd be in charge. I might like to think of myself as a badass, but this was way beyond my field of experience.

"What, you're not going to argue?" Matt sounded amused. I want to slap the look off his face.

"Arguing might get her killed," I replied. I shoved the chair away from the table and stood.

"Yes, it might." Matt shut the computer down and nodded to the admin staff before he steered me out of the room. "That might happen anyway. Nash might insist we not try to rescue her."

I stopped and stared at him. "I beg your pardon? We can't just leave her there."

Matt looked unapologetic. "If it means risking a few paranormals to save one normal, then we might have to. If it was my call—"

"Well, it's not," I snapped.

"And what if that's the call Nash makes?" Matt asked evenly.

"Then I'll go without you all." I resumed walking.

"You'll get yourself killed."

"Then you won't have to put up with me anymore," I told him. "I'm sure you'll be relieved."

He caught my arm and turned me to face him. "I would *not* be relieved." He searched my face with eyes laced with something I couldn't read. It almost seemed as if he cared or something. More than he'd let on.

"I don't want to see anyone die," he said finally. "Not even you."

"You said "especially you" wrong." I gave him a sarcastic smile.

He snorted. "You wish."

"Ha. Hardly." Okay, I did, but wish it a little bit, even though my hands were full enough with the guys who admitted they cared.

I pulled my arm back, but he held it firmly. "Here's where you let go so I don't kick you in the nuts," I said dryly.

"Well, if my nuts are at stake." He loosened his grip and stood back.

"Wise choice." I rubbed my arm. "I'd like to have a deep and meaningful conversation about why you looked at me the way you did, but my friend is currently being held hostage."

He rubbed his chin. "You imagined it, but yes, now is not the time. I trust you know where we're going?"

"Of course." I started toward Nash's room. "How do you know?"

"I make it my business to know."

"Some day you're going to have to explain a lot of things to me." I knocked on Nash's door.

"If you're alive to hear it, I might," Matt said, his voice tight.

I glanced over my shoulder in time to see that haunted look he got in his eyes. I knew Zeta had done something to him, but I didn't know what. I suspected he'd been born in a lab and had tests run on him for at least a part of his life. I had no idea what else they had done or even how he had escaped that existence. I was sure Zeta wanted him as much as they wanted me.

"I'll be alive all right," I assured him. "I'll survive if only to hear your backstory."

"I'm flattered." Matt gave me a funny look. He might have said more, but Nash's door swung open.

Nash gave me a hungry look, but it was quickly doused when he saw Matt as well. "I guess this is business," he said quietly. He ushered us inside and closed the door before he kissed me deeply.

"No offence, but this is important." Matt sounded unimpressed.

"So is this," I retorted, but I stepped away from Nash and leaned my hip against the table. I told Nash everything we knew.

"Show me the photo." Nash held out his hand for

my phone. He peered at the text and frowned. "It's nowhere I know either. Did you try to trace it?"

I frowned at him, then at Matt.

"It wasn't sent with magic." Matt shrugged. "I'm not familiar with the use of normal's tracking software."

"We'll have to rectify that," Nash told him. "In the meantime, call them." He handed the phone back to me.

Trembling, I took it and opened my contacts. "Are you sure? This might provoke them."

"It might," Nash agreed, "but it's most likely what they're waiting for. Until we make contact, we don't know what they want."

"We know exactly what they want," I said bitterly. "They want us all under their control." They wanted to use me and my magic to breed hybrids. My stomach twisted into a knot.

"We'll make sure that doesn't happen," Nash said fiercely. A flash of green lit his eyes, but it was gone a heartbeat later. I suspected, given half a chance, he'd shift into his dragon form and blast Zeta off the face of the planet. If I thought it was that simple, I might let him. It wouldn't be simple though. All his retaliation would do was slow them down a little and destroy him.

I exhaled deeply and pressed on Jess' number. The phone rang. And rang. Just when I thought it would ring out, it clicked.

My heart kicked into overdrive.

"Hello?" I said into my phone. "Who's there? Jess?"

"Peyton?" Her voice on the other end of the line was tiny.

"Jess! Are you all right?" I lifted frantic eyes to Nash's face. He looked so calm it was almost contagious. Almost. He gave me a nod and waved for me to keep talking.

"What have they done to you?" I asked. "Are you injured?"

"No, I'm okay." She spoke louder now, but high with obvious fear. "They want you to come here."

Of course they did. "Where are you?"

"They'll text you the address. They only want you to come."

"Right." I've seen enough movies to know how this goes. Arrive alone, tell no one, especially the cops. "When?"

The line was silent for a moment before she added, "They'll text that, too. They'll destroy the phone afterward so you can't call me again."

"I'll get you out of there," I assured her. "You're going to be fine. I promise."

"Peyton...don't come, save your—" The line went dead.

"Shit." I pressed the call button again, but no one answered. A couple of minutes later, a text popped up from her number.

Then...nothing.

I flopped down onto a chair and placed my phone on the table. It was that or throw it at the window in fear and frustration.

Nash stepped over, checked my phone, and made a note of the address they'd sent. "It's not far from here. They haven't given us much time to plan."

"Is there any point in me reminding you they said to come alone?" I asked wearily.

The guys exchanged looks.

"No," Matt said.

"None," Nash agreed. "Since Dyson and Kane are indisposed, it'll be just us. I don't think it's necessary to bring in Ariana or Hamish."

"It would be better to keep this small anyway," Matt said. "Just us three."

"I meant two," Nash said, "Peyton and I."

"Not a chance," Matt said immediately. "She might get you killed."

"She won't," Nash said firmly.

"No, I won't," I agreed. "I'm going alone."

"The hells you are," Nash growled. "If I have to tie you down to keep you from doing something crazy, I will."

"While that might be fun, I'm done putting everyone else in danger."

"We can take care of ourselves." Matt's face was slightly flushed. Was it all that talk about tying me down? "It's three of us or no one. If I have to, I'll go to the council and have them—"

Nash threw up his hands. "Fine, we're all going." He pointed a finger at Matt. "But if you ever threaten me again, it'll be the last thing you do here at the academy."

"That wasn't a threat," Matt replied coolly. "Just a matter of fact. I—"

"All right, can you stop?" I rubbed my temples. "Your dicks are about the same size, but if you want to pull them out and compare them, that's fine by me. In the meantime, make your plans and do it quickly. If Jess dies while you two are arguing—"

I sucked in a breath and wiped a tear off my cheek. I felt as though my life had started to implode, and it was dragging everyone else down with it. Maybe they'd be better off without me. They'd certainly be under less risk.

Okay, that was an assumption. Zeta had been

operating for longer than I had been alive. It would be around after I was gone, unless we could bring it down. I suspected all we would ever do was make a dent on their armour, but I sure as hells wasn't going to let them kill my best friend.

Nash nodded. "It'll be tricky, but here's what we do…"

20

"THIS IS A BAD IDEA," I muttered to myself. If I had a shred of sense, I would make myself invisible, ditch the guys and go after Jess by myself. What I lacked in sense, I made up for in reason. Both guys were hybrids. Both could do magic as well as shift. I needed their help. Besides, they'd kill me if I tried to lose them. Not literally. I hoped.

I approached the warehouse, eyes peeled for any movement. The place looked deserted. I know that was just for appearances, so no nosy people sniffed around. That would be the theory, at least. If I was looking for a hideout, or a place to live so I didn't have to sleep on the streets, this was exactly the kind of place I'd come to.

I sucked in a breath, squared my shoulders and

approached the small door on the side of the building. The only other entrance was a huge set of roller doors which looked locked down tight.

I half expected to be grabbed by an invisible witch or two before I even got near the door. My body was tensed for it. The only sound was that of my feet walking on gravel, and the whisper of wind. Every so often a car would pass, or a dog would bark in the distance. I heard no voices, no approaching army of invisible boots.

I stopped a metre from the door and listened again. Was this even the right place? The idea that this might be a wild goose chase occurred to me. They could have moved Jess to some other location by now. Hells, she might never have been here.

My skin tingled. The hair on the back of my neck rose. This was all kinds of wrong. Not just because I was risking my own life, but because at least three million things could go wrong with Nash's plan. Okay, maybe not that many, but I stopped counting after eleven.

"Who's there?" I called out.

No answer.

I rubbed my arm absently and stepped forward. My breath held, I tapped on the door. Once, twice, three times, just as instructed. The sound echoed inside the building, as though the whole place was empty.

The door swung open without a sound. Definitely not the rusty groan I was expecting. That in itself said a lot. How many not-so-deserted warehouses did Zeta have? How many contained hostages or paranormals held against their will?

"Hello?" I stepped closer, but not through the doorway yet.

Back out the street, a driver beeped their horn and I jumped.

"Bloody hells," I muttered. I was tense, obviously. Who wouldn't be in a situation like this? I glanced over my shoulder, but the car was already gone.

I counted to sixty, stepped inside the warehouse and made myself invisible.

Okay bastards, game on.

The room just inside the door must have been an office of some kind. A long desk was built into one wall. The door behind it was the only way into the rest of the building. It sat closed at the moment, but I heard raised voices beyond it. I stopped to listen but couldn't make out the words. The tone was obvious enough—they were angry.

Things which could go horribly wrong number five. The first four hadn't eventuated. Yet.

I held onto the magic while I clambered over the desk. I just managed to land silently on the other side when the door flew open. It clanged against the opposite wall and bounced back half-shut.

A familiar red-haired man stalked through the doorway.

Fitz.

"I know you're here, you fucking bitch," he snarled. "Show yourself!"

When he put it that way…

Even though he couldn't see it, I flipped him the finger and stepped lightly toward the door.

"I'm going to kill your friend." He turned a slow circle, hands raised, so I knew he had no idea where I was. "And then I'll make sure you're locked away, where you belong, in Zeta's laboratory."

I rolled my eyes at his tirade.

"Once you're safely in Zeta custody, I will make it my personal mission to break you."

Okay, now this guy was pissing me off. How much trouble had he gotten into for losing Dyson that he was so vindictive as a result? To be fair, he was a dick before the car crashed into the waterslide. Now he was an angry, vengeful dick.

I bit back a retort and snuck past him and through the door.

If he suspected anything, he gave no sign. He climbed onto the desk and jumped down the other side, muttering to me as he went.

On the other side of the door was a large room.

Jess sat tied to a chair, confused, but hopeful. Every so often her eyes would dart around as though she somehow knew I was there.

Several people in Zeta uniforms lay still on the ground nearby. Not dead, but unconscious for a while. Nash must have succeeded in reaching the roof and dumping a cylinder of gas into the air vents. The gas would only work on shifters, and only for a few hours, but it was enough. Thank the gods it worked on hybrids, too. On the other hand, the number of hybrids working for Zeta was breathtaking.

Only a handful of agents remained standing, or crouched beside hybrids. They might all be normals, but they might also be witches or wizards. This war went deeper than normals versus paranormals. It was more like...paranormals and normals who wanted the world under their heel and those who didn't.

I swallowed down my outrage and focused. Without knowing what I was dealing with, I had to be careful. Neither Matt nor Nash could help me until I got Jess clear of the building. That was the most difficult part of this plan, and the place where the most things could go wrong.

I stepped over closer to her, my steps as silent as I could make them.

Three metres.

Two metres.

One metre.

I dropped to a crouch behind her.

"Whatever you do, don't flinch," I whispered.

She startled slightly, but not enough to draw attention to herself. She lowered her head as if to nod and raised it again. She wriggled her hands, but they were bound hard with cable ties.

Of course, why couldn't it be rope, loosely knotted? Evil bastards.

I was ready for this, thanks to Matt, but I would have to act quickly.

Heart racing, I dropped my magic and conjured a small knife from the new tattoo on my wrist. It wouldn't last long, but it was sharp enough to cut through the ties.

They fell away just as one of the agents noticed my presence.

"She's here!" she shouted. She pulled out a gun and aimed it at Jess' head. "Don't move or I shoot."

"You won't shoot," I moved closer to Jess. "You might hit me. You know your boss wants me alive."

The agent hesitated.

I used the time to grab Jess' wrist and form a bubble around both of us.

The agent pulled the trigger.

I dropped to a crouch and pulled Jess down with me. The bullet sailed over both of our heads. Judging by the clang and subsequent echo, it slammed into the wall behind us. A small part of me regretted the fact it hadn't hit Fitz or someone like him. The rest of me didn't really want to see anyone dead, although better them than me and Jess.

"We have to be quiet and move slowly," I said in her ear.

She nodded and smiled in a way that made me feel like a fraud. She seemed so sure I was in control here, that I knew exactly what I was doing.

Girl, I don't have a clue.

I nodded toward the door and we rose, hand in hand.

Every Zeta agent was on their feet now, all alert for where we might be. A couple still had guns, but most now had tranquilliser guns in their hands. Barrels were aimed roughly in our direction, but they waited.

One little mistake and we would… Shit, I needed to sneeze.

No, that was *not* a part of this plan.

I screwed up my face and pinched my nose with the fingers of my spare hand.

The sneeze receded, but I knew that trick. The moment I lowered my hand, it would come back, twice as hard.

I held my breath and pulled Jess along a little faster.

Unfortunately faster meant Jess accidentally scuffed her shoe on the floor. The sound was tiny, but enough to be heard.

Half a dozen Zeta tranquilliser darts flew toward us.

I pulled Jess down again, but not before a dart struck her arm.

She let out a tiny squeak, but bit her lip to keep from making any more noise.

I tugged her to her feet and hurried toward the door. I needed to get her out, over the desk and out to where Nash and Matt waited. All before the dart took effect.

No pressure.

"You should save yourself," she said in my ear.

"I'm not leaving without you," I said, mouthing

most of the words. I hadn't come all this way to leave her behind. "Just a little further."

I pulled her into the office.

She started to slump slightly. "I don't feel so…"

"We're nearly there." I hesitated. How the hells was I going to get us both over the desk? I thought for a moment.

"You go over first. I'll keep the magic going and give you a shove if you need one." Easy to say. Doing it…that might be different.

She nodded and leaned against the desk. She managed to raise one leg high enough to place on the desk, but I had to push her up the rest of the way. Once there, she closed her eyes and sagged.

Shit.

"Jess?" I shook her, but she didn't wake.

Okay, I can do this. Somehow.

With one hand on her, I climbed up, trying hard not to put too much weight on her. With all the elegance of a hippopotamus, but hopefully none of the noise, I jumped off the other side of the desk.

Right, easy. Now, to pick her up somehow. I glanced toward the door. What I needed right now was to have Nash or Matt come running in, ready to help. I was a kickass woman, but I would struggle to lift someone who weighed a bit more than I did.

They didn't come.

Okay, improvisation time.

I could... No, that wouldn't work. *Maybe I if I...* Nope, bad idea.

Fuckity fuck, every idea I had involved making too much noise, or making myself visible. I was getting tired from holding magic for so long, but I couldn't just leave Jess here.

I chewed my lip.

I had no choice. I grabbed her under her arms and pulled her down from the desk. Her feet hit the floor with a thud that drew the Zeta agents to the door.

"We know you're there. You have nowhere to go."

I ignored them and dragged Jess over to the door. If we could just slip out...

A shadow fell over us both.

"Going somewhere?"

I glanced over my shoulder and dropped my magic in surprise.

Dyson stood beside Fitz.

Dyson aimed a tranquilliser gun at me.

21

"WHAT THE HELLS?" I raised my hands. "Dyson, what are you doing?"

I noticed then his eyes were glazed.

"He's doing whatever he's told," Fitz said with a smile. "Just like you'll learn to do."

"You've drugged him," I said. My eyes never left Dyson.

He blinked. I was sure I saw him deep inside, trying to fight this—whatever they had done to him. Maybe if I could buy him some time…

"In a manner of speaking," Fitz replied. "Now, we can do this one of two ways. You walk to the car I have waiting outside and get in, or your boyfriend here will put you to sleep and drag you in there for me."

"I don't like either of those options," I said, calm on the outside, mind and heart racing on the inside. "How about you leave us alone? Things aren't going to end well for you if you keep working for Zeta." He'd be lucky if Nash bit his head off cleanly.

"On the contrary, I'll be very well rewarded when we bring you in." He looked so smug, I wanted to punch him in the face.

"What I don't get is why," I said. "Why me? There are tons of witches out there who are more power-ful, skilled, and probably better looking. Seriously, if this is about my mother, then maybe take it out with her. We're not that close. If Zeta thinks I would be a good bargaining chip—"

"Enough." He made a slicing gesture with his hand. "Maybe if I kill your friend, you'll understand I'm serious." He turned his gun toward Jess.

"An innocent woman who can't even fight back," I said in disgust. "Your balls must be tiny."

I saw the bullet leave the gun before I registered the sound of it going off.

"No!" The word tore from my throat.

The bullet slammed into the ground a hair from Jess' head.

"Next time, I'll put a bullet in her brain," Fitz said

coldly. "Get in the car and she can wake up here, alone but alive. Resist and she dies. Your choice."

My heart was in my throat. I had no doubt he meant what he said. I had come too fucking close to getting her killed. I glanced toward Dyson, but his expression was blank. Whatever they had given him, it was in control at the moment.

"Fine, I'll co-operate." Part of me wanted to see if Dyson would pull the trigger, but I didn't dare to risk being asleep for hours. I believed what Fitz had said about breaking me. I wouldn't let him touch me without a fight.

"If you hurt her in *any* way…"

Fitz gestured toward the door with his gun. "You're in no position to make threats."

I opened my mouth to point out I had friends in the vicinity, but shut it again. He would know I had help, because someone put all the hybrids to sleep, but he probably didn't know both guys were out there.

I brushed past Dyson on the way out the door, but his body was stiff. The drug was winning, for now.

I wished I believed all of that. Kane was smart, but Zeta could have spent years on it. It might take him that long to work out what it was, much less what to do about it. Dyson could be like this forever. The idea choked me up. What would they ask him to do to me? My stomach churned.

"Open the door," Fitz barked at one of the Zeta agents who stood near the SUV. Black, of course, just like Fitz's soul.

She jumped to tug the door open and stepped aside as if I was some kind of wild animal. I bared my teeth at her, just to see her flinch.

"I've changed my mind," Fitz said just before I climbed into the car. "She's too dangerous to keep awake. Dyson, tranq her."

I whirled around. "But I said I would cooperate."

"And I don't believe you." Fitz nodded to Dyson.

Dyson's hand twitched. A flash of apology crossed his eyes.

I shook my head. "Don't do it. You can fight this. You're stronger than whatever they've given you."

He looked pained. "Don't...want...to..." He squeezed the trigger. The dart flew out of the barrel and hit my shoulder.

"Ouch! Fucking hells." I gripped it and yanked it free before throwing it to the ground. It clattered before it came to a stop at Fitz's feet. Empty.

Shit.

"Get into the car." Fitz ordered.

I raised my chin. Where the hells were Nash and Matt? This would have been the perfect moment for them to sweep in and do a bit of clawing and biting.

My eyelids were heavy already. My body insisted I lie down and sleep. I fought the urge.

"Get her into the car," Fitz ordered.

Dyson moved forward and pushed me inside. "Sorry," he said, his voice groggy. Or was that my head?

"You have to keep fighting," I told him. At least, I think I did. I wasn't sure if the words passed my lips.

He lifted my legs and placed them on the seat.

I caught sight of Fitz's amused face before the door slammed shut, followed by my eyes.

I AWOKE IN A COOL, dark room. That was a small mercy because my head pounded like someone hammered a nail into my temple. I opened my eyes a crack.

I lay on a narrow bed in what looked like the laboratory at UA. Was there any point in hoping that was where I was? The guys could have swept in and rescued Dyson and I while I had a little nap.

I raised my head, but winced and put it back down when the pain increased.

Gods, it hurt. I squeezed my eyes shut and rolled onto my side. Nothing felt broken and I was still wearing the same clothes I'd had on when I fell asleep.

I opened my eyes again. I was almost certain I wasn't at UA. At least I was alive.

For now.

I rolled over onto my back and stared at the ceiling. It was only then I noticed a bandage on my left arm. Tentatively I touched it.

Son of a bitch. I was almost certain it was right where my birth control was. Or, if I guessed right, had been.

I shivered. Were they really serious about using me to make hybrids? Between that realisation and the pain in my head, my stomach turned. I rolled over and threw up on their pristine, white floor. Shame it wasn't Fitz's shoes, or someone equally nasty.

"Ah, you're awake." A soft voice spoke from the doorway. "Don't try to use magic, it'll hurt like the blazes."

The speaker was a woman around my age. Her eyes were rimmed in dark shadows and her belly was heavily swollen. Something about her was familiar, but I couldn't put my finger on it.

I forced myself to sit up. "They're so badass they sent a pregnant woman to make sure I behave?" My tone wasn't even slightly friendly.

She stepped inside and gave me a bitter smile. "I think the idea is to show you that you can't win. No matter how much you fight." Her hand went to her belly. She looked as though she might cry.

"They think I won't blast you out of the way and escape?" I said coldly. I had no reason to believe she wasn't on Zeta's side. There had to be some women willing to make hybrids for them. She might just as easily be one.

"If you do, then at least make sure I can't get up again." She looked away. She was so convincing I almost believed her. Part of me wanted to.

I frowned, but instantly regretted it. I waited until the worst of the throbbing in my forehead receded before I spoke again. "How do I know you're not one of them?"

She hesitated, then shrugged. "You don't, but I'm not. I was like you, young and full of fight. After the first baby—"

"First... How many have you had?"

She swallowed audibly. "This is the third. They might let me see this one, if I can convince you to do as they ask."

I gaped. My stomach rolled again. "I'm not going to just..." Gods, if they thought I would just let them violate me and not fight with everything I had...

She sniffed. "I didn't think you would. Why would you? But it will make them work twice as hard to break you. Personally I think some of them prefer it."

"Some of them?" I echoed. "How many?"

She shrugged. "Enough."

"Hybrids?"

"Sometimes," she agreed. "Sometimes it's just a needle with shifter DNA. Those are better. Easier."

"Yeah, it would be." A needle versus getting raped. What a choice.

"If you're lucky, that's all you'll get. It's more reliable that way. Higher chance of impregnation with the right combination of DNA. So they said anyway." She rubbed her belly again.

"That's what they did with you the last time?" I asked.

She nodded. "They're trying to make a dragon

hybrid. They're hard to make. If this works, they'll do it again."

And again and again until they wore her out. She didn't need to say any of that, it was written on her face.

"Right." Would they try that with me? If Nash fathered my child, we might have done that naturally. Ironic. Zeta could have simply waited a few years. We might have done it on our own.

"They seem to be especially interested in me," I said softly. "Have you got any idea why? Why did they want you, of all the witches?"

She blinked. "It was something about my blood. I don't really know."

I rubbed my aching forehead with my fingertips. All of this thinking was painful and tiring. "I'm just a witch. My parents are just a witch and a wizard. There's nothing unique about me."

"Perhaps there is and you didn't know?" she suggested.

"That's possible," I said doubtfully, "but I have no idea how Zeta would know."

"They will have taken your blood." She pointed to my bandage. "They might tell you, if you cooperate with them."

There she was again, asking me to be good. As if that would happen.

"We'll see." I lowered my hands. "What's your name?"

She hesitated. "Thora."

"Peyton." I held my hand out to her. "I wish we'd met under better circumstances."

"Me too." She shook my hand, but looked over her shoulder while she did it. "I should go."

"Yes, you should," Fitz agreed as he stepped through the door. He jerked his head at her.

She gave me a wide eyed look, but hurried out as quickly as a heavily pregnant woman could waddle.

Fitz closed the door behind her and locked it. "Try to do magic."

"Why should I?" I remembered Thora telling me it would hurt.

"Aren't you going to defend yourself?" He stepped closer.

I shivered at the look in his eyes. I squinted and felt around for magic in the room and outside it. The moment I touched some in the metal of the door-frame, a searing pain flashed through my head.

I cried out and dropped the magic immediately.

Fitz chuckled and stepped closer while I waited for the agony to recede.

"Big man, huh?" I choked out. "You need to incapacitate a woman to feel good about yourself."

"Zeta has blocked your access to magic," he said easily, "but you're far from helpless. I'm sure you have lots of fight left." His tongue darted over his lips. He grabbed my arm in a tight grip.

"I look forward to *pounding* it out of you."

2 2

I GRITTED MY TEETH. "And risk me having a *normal* baby? No offence, asshole, but your hair is bright red. No one would miss the resemblance."

Fitz smirked. "What risk? That birth control will be in your system for days, possibly longer. Besides, there's more than one way to prevent pregnancy."

"Yeah, like celibacy," I retorted. "Or losing your nuts." I aimed my knee but he grabbed it and used that and my arm to slam me to the floor.

Fuck, that was a stupid, rookie mistake. If I wasn't still groggy from the tranquilliser, I might not have made it.

While I was still catching my breath, he straddled me and pinned my arms above my head. The smile he gave me was one of contempt.

"I thought you'd fight harder than that."

"Sorry to disappoint you," I said sarcastically. "Let me up and we can have a do-over."

"Tempting." He ran a hand down my side and across my belly. "Maybe we can do that next time."

"Well, that's something to look forward to, isn't it?" I didn't move while he touched me, not even a twitch. I suspected he got off on women struggling. The more I fought to get free, the more excited he'd become. And the more violent he might get.

He tugged my shirt up and pinched my nipple through my bra.

I forced myself not to react.

"Tough girl, hmmm?" He twisted my nipple until tears sprang to my eyes.

I clenched my teeth. At least the pain in my head lessened in comparison to this.

"Maybe you like it rough," he suggested. "You enjoy a little pain?" He twisted the other way until a cry involuntarily escaped my lips.

He grinned.

I swore then and there I was going to kill him. Quickly, slowly, it didn't matter. I wanted him to look me in the eyes and know his life was ending, and I was doing it. My stomach rebelled. I had never wanted to hurt anyone before, but he was a sadistic bastard. Had he violated Thora? I would almost bet on it.

"Good," he said smoothly, "get angry."

I wanted to spit in his face, but I bit back my fury.

He reached for the button of my jeans. While he tried to work it free, he loosened his grip on my wrists.

With a grunt, I rolled us and drove a knee into his groin.

He let out a cry of rage but rolled me onto my back before he pinned me with the length of his body.

His eyes watered, but he growled. "Fucking bitch, you'll pay for that." The pain in his voice gave me some satisfaction.

Not as much as I got from slamming the heel of my hand into his face.

He rolled off me and staggered to his feet, his hands over his nose. He turned and kicked me hard in the side as I tried to get back to my feet.

"Bitch. I'm going to break you so hard you'll beg me to kill you."

Before he could say another word, or act on his threat, the door swung open.

A man and a woman in laboratory coats stepped inside.

"Agent Fitz." The man gave him a look, as though he knew what the man had been up to. I couldn't tell what his opinion of it was though.

"Dr Yates. Dr Taylor." Fitz nodded. "Watch this one. She attacked me."

"Unprovoked?" Yates asked over his clipboard.

"I was simply trying to explain her place in this program," Fitz lied.

"I see." Yates nodded. "Perhaps you should have your nose seen to."

"Right." Fitz shot me a dirty look before he hurried from the room.

"That man," Taylor muttered once the door was closed again. "His temper will be a liability some day."

"But it would have been fine if he was a hybrid?" I snapped.

Yates placed his clipboard on the bed and crossed his arms. "The change to insemination by needle was a slow one, but ultimately beneficial to—"

"You're using witches as breeding cows," I growled. "Why do you care if it's a needle or a cock? It's a violation either way."

Taylor turned her face away.

"You're even worse," I told her. "You're letting it happen to other women."

"For the good of humanity," she muttered. "I've borne five children for the cause myself."

I shook my head. "You folk are sick."

"Be that as it may," Yates said, "we can't take the chance you'll be damaged."

"I'm glad my wellbeing is so important to you," I said bitterly.

"Yes, well, today we merely have questions," Yates said.

"Fuck off," I replied.

Yates ignored my response. "Why were you immune to the gas which immobilises shifters?"

I frowned. "Because I'm not a shifter." Wasn't that obvious?

"Oh, but you are a hybrid," Taylor said.

I blinked and shook my head. "I beg your pardon?"

Taylor repeated herself.

"I think I would know if I could shift."

"You may not be able to," Yates said. "Or at least, not yet. It was always going to be a question for second generation hybrids. Your father—"

I jerked my gaze back toward him. "What the hells? What does *he* have to do with this?" I rubbed my forehead. The ache was only dull now, but my head was spinning.

"You father is a hybrid," Taylor said, as if I should know that already.

I shook my head. "No, he's not. He's a wizard. Just an ordinary wizard."

"You're mistaken." Yates glanced down at his clipboard. "He's a phoenix."

"You two are out of your minds." I stepped back and sagged back against the wall. "I think I would know if my father was anything like that." After two had tried to kill me, I wasn't a huge fan of the giant birds, but the idea my father might be one was laughable. He hardly ever did magic, much less shift and fly around.

"Your father became embittered with Zeta and convinced your mother to leave. That was before you were born. Zeta paired them in the hope of creating…well, you."

Taylor nodded. "Zeta has been trying to work with you ever since. Your mother has been reluctant."

"You knew where I was, my whole life?" I guessed. When Taylor nodded, I asked, "Why wait until now?"

"We hoped your mother would bring you to us willingly," Yates said. "As a member of the board of Zeta, she—"

"What the *absolute fuck?*" There was my stomach, threatening to empty again. "She is *not.*"

"Oh, but she is," Yates said. "She chose not to take further part in the breeding program, but she understands the importance."

"Wait." I took a moment for several long breaths. "My mother knows witches are being raped and bred?"

Taylor looked uncomfortable. "As I said, the needle—"

"Is still rape!" I raged. "Women are forced to have children they don't even get to meet." I couldn't believe my *mother* would have any part of it. Tears stung my eyes. I shook my head. "I don't believe she would allow it to happen. Does she know I'm here?"

"Not yet. She'll be informed when we've finished testing you."

"She won't let you keep me here," I said weakly.

"We have that time to convince you of the importance of the program," Yates said.

"By that you mean break me until I have no strength left to argue."

Neither denied it.

I sucked in a breath. "What did you mean when you said she would take no further part?"

They exchanged a glance. "That's something you should ask her."

"I'm asking you," I said coldly.

Taylor sighed. "She had two children before you. The first was stillborn. The second…"

"What?" I had siblings? This was becoming too much to process. I sucked in a breath to slow my mind a little. "What was wrong with the second?"

"Not wrong, exactly," Taylor said slowly. "She was a chimera. Technically she still is."

"She's alive," I said softly.

"Yes, but she doesn't see other people," Taylor said. "She's a danger to herself and others."

"She wants you Zeta assholes dead too, hmm?" I had zero sympathy for any of them. Let her rip their heads off.

"She almost killed your parents," Yates said dryly. "She can't control herself when she shifts, that was part of the reason your mother stopped breeding." He shrugged one shoulder. "She had you anyway."

"Yes, me, just a regular witch with no ability to shift."

"But with hybrid DNA," Yates said insistently. "And yet, the immunity I mentioned earlier. You're unique. Valuable."

He sounded so covetous, I took a step away from him. "That's what this is all about, isn't it? You knew what I was and you want to see what kind of babies I'll make. Well let me tell you, I won't play your sick games."

"Oh, you will. You're too important to the cause for us to let you do otherwise." Yates picked up his clipboard.

"We could find out what happens when a second generation hybrid breeds with a human," Taylor said coldly.

I swallowed at her thinly veiled threat. "What happened to your precious needles?"

"Whatever it takes to bend you to our way of thinking," she said.

"Bend," I said slowly, "or break?"

She shrugged indifferently.

Gods, these people were monsters. "And if I choose to go along with your shitty plan, then what?"

"Shifter DNA," Taylor replied. "We have been experimenting with dog DNA. The results are fascinating. I believe you're acquainted with Dyson? Your impregnation could be quite...pleasurable."

"Considering you had to drug him to get him to cooperate, I doubt that," I said dryly. I had thought about having children with Dyson some day, but it involved a whole lot of consent.

"I suspect bird DNA would be a better match for phoenix DNA," Taylor went on. "That was how it began after all. We know you have a bird more than happy to copulate with you."

I started. "How did you know about that?" Gods, don't tell me they were standing outside the window on one or both occasions? "Don't tell me, you have an informant at UA?"

They exchanged glances again.

"Not exactly, no," Yates replied. "Not in the way you're thinking. Zeta runs the University of Arcana."

If he'd told me I could shift into a three-headed, pink rhinoceros I couldn't have been more surprised.

"The evil government organisation who wants to kill shifters and enslave witches, runs a university for paranormals? You know shifters go there, right?" Under other circumstances I might have laughed, especially at the thought of Xav's face when he found out. His precious UA was more a danger to him than I had ever been. What a trip. Pun intended.

"Of course. It's an excellent source of recruits and knowledge," Yates replied.

I swallowed. Did Nash know about this? Did

Matt? Surely they didn't, or they would have made sure I was as far away from the place as possible.

"Kane is studying science. He worked in the lab." He studied the very things they might use against us.

Yates confirmed that with a nod. "His findings have been very useful. Especially in helping us to discern how long the shifter control drug actually works. Thanks to him, we knew to increase the dosage. With help, we'll make the effects longer lasting."

"He would hate it if he knew he was helping you," I hissed.

"He might. Until we offer him a lot of money to help us. When you tell him you've decided to cooperate, that will sweeten the deal."

I crossed my arms. "I won't ever tell him that."

"You will, we'll make sure of that," Taylor said. She seemed almost bored, as if she'd held this conversation a hundred times before. They were certain they'd beat me because they beat gods knew how many others before.

"I want to see my mother," I demanded. There was no way she'd let them do any of this to me, if she knew I was here.

"In time," Taylor said with a nod. "Behave and

that time will come sooner. If you decide to be diffi-cult...you'll wish we let Fitz have you."

"I would never wish for that," I said firmly. Gods, what did they have that was worse than being violated by someone like him?

23

LEFT ALONE, I had nothing but time to consider everything they had told me. I would take it all with a grain of salt. Hells, a whole fucking barrel of it.

I slumped against the wall on the other side of the room and watched the door while my brain turned over and over. At least my stomach settled. For now.

Methodically, I teased out everything they had said, bit by bit. The first was the suggestion I had two sisters. I'd never laboured under the illusion my mother wanted me particularly much. This would explain why, but a dozen other things would as well, including her busy schedule. A schedule I was almost certain didn't include being on the board of an evil organisation. Surely she would know all about Zeta's involvement in the UA and stop me from going?

I ran a hand over my hair.

She tried, but I ignored her. I put it down to some kind of maternal need to protect me, but if it was my kid, I would have locked her in her room until she came to her senses.

I snorted to myself. She probably would have done just that if there was a chance of it working. I would have broken out and left anyway. She knew that. I was nothing if not headstrong.

Still, none of that meant she was involved with Zeta. Gods, they tried to kill us last year. There was no way…

I shook my head, but the seed of doubt had sprouted already.

Okay, so maybe I had a dangerous, living sister and an evil mother. What about my father? It sounded as though he might be involved in this up to his eyeballs as well. That was the hardest thing to swallow. My father was the most kind, gentle, decent man I knew. He wouldn't have locked me up, he would have sat me down and explained everything. Assuming he knew.

I chewed my lip. Or would he? Was it possible he really was an actual hybrid and had never told me?

That seemed like the kind of thing you tell your child.

Hey, kiddo, you might shift some day, because I can. And by the way, I met your mother in a lab. We bonded over a nice bottle of DNA and an IV.

I snorted to myself. The truth was, I didn't know what was the truth. It was possible every word the agents said was a lie, designed to make me do exactly what I was doing, freaking out. I needed to stop and think about what I knew to be fact.

Fact, Kane cared about me and he would never play along with their sick games, unless they drugged him. Same with Dyson.

Fact, Nash also cared about me and he was probably out there planning to break me out of here. Same with Matt, even if he wouldn't admit it.

Fact, Ariana—I winced, I almost forgot about her. My mother arranged for her and Matt to keep an eye on me. By leaving her out of Jess' attempted rescue, we kept her safe from this. For that I was grateful, although including her might have increased the chance of success. Maybe I wouldn't be sitting here right now, waiting for…

I stopped myself before I spiralled into a black hole.

"Fact, I'm a badass," I muttered. I could wait for them to take me or I could get myself out of here.

Tentatively, I tried to draw magic again. The searing pain wasn't quite as bad as the first time, but it still sucked.

Fine, old fashioned escape plan it was then.

I rose and tweaked aside the curtain which hung over the small window.

Barred. No surprise there.

I grabbed two of them and pulled.

Nothing. Whoever put them in place intended them to stay there. I doubted even a blast of magic would make them budge. Even if they would, the drop once I got out the window would probably kill me. Unless I was an actual phoenix, but on the way to my death was no time to test that theory.

I peered out, just in case a dragon hovered outside the window.

Nope, just a whole lot of blue sky and trees.

That left the door, but leaving through a building full of Zeta agents would be difficult, even with magic.

I tried the knob, but the door was locked, as I expected. I could try to kick the door down, but it looked as solidly made as the bars.

"Fuck you, good workmanship," I muttered. Why

couldn't this place have been made by a cowboy builder? It was the government, for the gods' sake, they were all about cutting corners.

Apparently not today.

I looked up for a vent, skylight, anything I could climb into. The ceiling was unbroken except for the lights and they were too small for anything but a flea.

"Ladies and gentlemen," I said under my breath, "the situation was looking difficult for your hero, but she's not giving up yet." *She is, however, talking to herself.*

The door clicked and swung open. I had to force down the urge to jump back, especially when I saw Fitz's bandaged face and furious eyes. I wasn't sure if the two armed agents with him were a good thing or a very bad thing.

"This way." He jerked his head toward the corridor.

Rule number one, never let a potential attacker take you somewhere else. Did that rule even apply here? I didn't know, but I didn't immediately comply.

"Why?" I asked instead.

His face turned pink. Not a cute pink like Kane, but an ugly, blotchy pink.

"Move," he snarled.

"Have you ever tried saying please?" I asked.

"You enjoyed being tranquillised that much?" he replied.

I only paused for a moment longer before I stepped out of the room. I couldn't risk being asleep around a vengeful man like Fitz.

"Where are we going?" I asked cheerfully. I walked behind one of the agents, with Fitz and the other behind me. I took note of every turn we made until we reached the elevator and waited.

"You'll see. Keep your mouth shut." Fitz poked me in the side with his gun, right in the spot he'd kicked me.

I winced. Through watering eyes, I saw him smile.

Fucker.

"I guess your nose is broken." I peered at it.

Blotchy pink turned to blotchy red. I suspected if we were alone, he would have struck me across the face. As it was, he poked me again in the same place.

"If you know what's good for you, you'll keep your mouth shut," he growled.

"Is he always so grumpy?" I asked one of the other agents, a man with curly hair. I knew to move away from Fitz before he could touch me again.

The elevator pinged and the door slid open.

"The last time I was in an elevator with Zeta agents, they both ended up dead," I remarked. "Are you sure you want to take that risk?"

"Inside," Curly instructed. "No one needs to die today."

"He does." I nodded toward Fitz. "He's a nasty piece of—"

Fitz took a swing at my face, but I ducked and he missed. He staggered forward a few steps.

"See what I mean?" I said to Curly. "That would have hurt."

"Keep your mouth shut and it won't happen again." Curly ushered me inside the elevator.

"Victim blaming much?" I muttered. I eyed the last agent, a woman with wheat-blonde hair and striking blue eyes. I couldn't tell what she was thinking about any of this.

I leaned against the side of the elevator, arms crossed, every bit of me as far from Fitz as I could get.

The elevator moved down. Two floors. Three. Four. Five.

It stopped on the twelfth floor. I know, I would have guessed they'd take me to the thirteenth too, but maybe they were superstitious.

"Out, please." Curly nodded.

I immediately moved to comply. "See where having manners gets you?"

For some reason, Curly smiled at that. He would have been cute if not for the whole evil organisation thing.

"To the right," Fitz barked. He led the way down the corridor.

I felt safer behind him, with Curly and the woman on either side of me. Safe, of course, was a relative term. I was far from safe, really.

Fitz pulled out a card, slid it through the reader beside a door and pushed it open.

"Inside."

I hesitated. If I stepped into this room, I would be locked in again. I had already determined that only led to being trapped.

"Please." Curly sounded amused.

Fitz shot him a dark look, but Curly shrugged and gestured for me to precede him into the room.

I sighed and took a step forward.

A ringtone broke the silence of the corridor and Fitz swore. He pulled a phone out of his pocket.

"Blake, get the bitch inside and ready for the doctors." He stalked off down the corridor, the phone to his ear.

"Saved by the bell," Curly said with a smile.

"Blake..." the woman said, her tone clearly a warning.

"No, Corinne, it's time." Blake grabbed my arm and pulled me into the room.

Corinne followed and closed the door behind us.

I managed to jerk my arm from Blake and turned to face him, hands up, ready to fight back. Had I traded one wannabe rapist for another?

"It's okay." Blake put his gun away and raised his own hands. "We won't hurt you. We work for the council. We're here to help you."

Corinne sighed and put her own gun away. "I told you you're too soft for this undercover stuff. The first pretty face and you fold."

Blake shrugged and held out his hand. "I'm Blake Jordan. This is my cousin Corinne." He smiled, forming a dimple in his cheek.

"I knew you were too cute to be a baddie," I said without thinking.

Blake laughed. "I don't know about that."

Corinne snorted. "Yes you do and you know it. Now stop wasting time, we need to get out of here."

"About that." I pointed toward the door. "We're in enemy territory here. There's some kind of dampening field on magic."

They exchanged nods. "We need to bring down that field and get the witches out of here. We need your help for that."

"Hey, I'm as badass as the next girl—" Corinne did seem pretty badass, "but they have guns, tranquillisers and the numbers."

"And we have a phoenix," Corinne said softly.

It took a moment to realise she was talking about me.

I shook my head. "I know they think that, but I've never shifted in my life."

"They brought you here for that," Corinne said.

I looked around the room now. It was another lab, this one bigger than the one at UA by at least twice.

"They've developed a formula to make shifters shift."

I blinked, but it made sense. They would have been searching for a way to stop them. Perhaps they'd stumbled upon the opposite during their research.

"So you want me to take it?" I grimaced. None of this seemed like a good idea to me.

When Blake nodded, I added, "And what if it doesn't work?"

"Then we'll try plan b," Blake said.

"There is no plan b," Corinne said.

Blake looked at her sharply. "There isn't?"

She shook her head. "No, just plan a. They were sure this would work. I wasn't going to try this yet, but bringing you here has forced our hand." She frowned at Blake.

He shrugged. "It felt right."

"So, if I'm not a shifter, we go straight to plan f?" I asked. "As in, we're fucked."

24

"How horrible is this going to taste and why should I trust either of you?" I frowned at the vial of white, cloudy liquid.

"Do you want the answers to those in that order?" Blake asked.

I held the vial to the side so I could look at him through one eye. "Either way is fine."

"You can trust us," Corinne said quickly. "But even if you don't, they'd make you drink that anyway. If Fitz were here, he'd tie you down first, just in case."

"Right." I could just imagine what else that would entail.

"This way we can be ready when he comes back."

Blake glanced meaningfully toward the door. "He won't be much longer."

"Did you organise that phone call?" I asked.

"I wish." Blake leaned against a workbench. "That was just dumb luck."

"Speak for yourself," Corinne said.

Blake gave her a surprised glance, but his expression quickly changed to impressed. "Nice."

Corinne shrugged. "Drink up. I'm going to pull my gun so it looks like we're forcing you into it." She nodded at Blake to do the same.

The doorknob turned.

I opened the vial and gulped down the contents. It tasted like the kind of medicine you usually take from a needle, not by mouth.

"Ugh, disgusting. Leave it to you evil people to make everything taste like crap." I stuck out my tongue and gave Blake a look as if I still assumed he was on Fitz's side.

The door opened. Fitz stepped inside. He stopped, took in the scene and his mouth twitched to the side.

"She should be bound," he said coolly. "For her own protection." He stalked toward me and pulled a cable tie out of his pocket.

I shit you not. Apparently he carried them

around with him like he thought he might need one at any moment.

"No need." I held up a hand. "I told you I'm not a shifter." My hand turned blue and sprouted feathers. Where a moment ago I'd had an arm, I now had a wing.

"Fuck."

At least that's what I would have said if I had a mouth and not a beak.

Apparently they were right.

That was the last coherent thought I had before my mind became a tumult of emotion and sensation. I had wings.

I could fly.

I had been lied to.

I could rip Fitz's head off.

I started toward him.

Eyes wide with fear, he backed toward the door. "Get the tranquilliser!" His voice was so high I thought his balls might have retreated into his body. "Use it on the bitch!"

I lifted a foot… No, giant, taloned claws.

I stared at them for a moment, then shredded Fitz from the top of his head right down to his calves. He didn't even have time to let out a squeak.

Blood rained out of him, covered the floor. Gore stained my claws.

I let out a bird-like squawk. The phoenix part of me revelled in the smell of blood, the joy of killing. The rest of me was shoved so far back into my head I could barely register my own existence. All I wanted was to kill again.

I turned toward the other agents. Stalked toward them.

One shouted something, but I couldn't make it out. It didn't matter, I just wanted to kill.

"Peyton!"

What was that? *Who* was that? Who dared to try to break through to me? I was a phoenix, made to destroy. Made to burn the world down.

"It's me, Dyson. I fought back. Now *you* have to."

Dyson? Did I know that name?

I swung around. He stood near the door. I sensed the warmth of his body.

I stepped toward him. I was a creature of fire. I needed to take his heat, to leave him cold. When they were all cold, I would burn what was left and then burn the ashes.

"Peyton! You need to shift back to yourself," Dyson called out. "It's hard the first time, but you can do it. You don't want to hurt anyone else."

I hissed. Yes I did. Why didn't he understand that?

I shook my head. My mind was a jumble. All I could think of was death. No, it was more than that. I wanted to be sure I'd done the job right.

I stopped over to Fitz's corpse and tore his mangled head from his shoulders with my beak. I spat on the floor, leaving a splatter of blood and saliva. Let that be a warning to them all not to fuck with me.

I shook my beak. Droplets of blood flew everywhere, but my thoughts were clearer now.

"Come back to me," he urged. "I love you. We need you to be you so we can all get out of here."

Out of here. The words resonated. Dyson was wrong, they didn't need me in witch form, they needed me like this.

I tried to speak, but my shifter form wouldn't make words. I put a clawed foot to my head instead.

"The dampening field." Corinne appeared in front of me and nodded. "It's a level down." Specks of blood coated her cheek, but she didn't seem to notice. At least it wasn't hers. Thanks to Dyson, I came back to myself in time.

I tapped at the floor with a claw while I thought.

I wasn't going to fit in the elevator like this, but I had to bring down that field.

I bobbed my head and stepped over to the window. What a dragon could do, surely a phoenix could as well.

I gripped the bars in my claws and tore them clean out of the wall. With barely a heave, I tossed them through the window and jumped out after them.

Okay, here's the bit where I should have practiced flying first. I plunged like a stone for several floors until I managed to throw out my arms and catch myself.

I flapped like crazy and rose back to the twelfth floor. Dyson all but hung out the window.

"That's my girl." He grinned.

I let out a little creel and dropped the floor below. As easily as before, I tore the bars off the window and threw them into the room.

The three or four occupants screamed and ran for the door. I thought about killing them. I *wanted* to, but if they ended up being on my side…

I let them go and turned toward a panel on the side of the room. I had expected to find a mechanism attached to the brain of a witch, or at least some kind of complicated machinery.

Instead, a large, black stone, like a huge pearl, sat in the centre of the panel. I heard about witches using stones, but I had never seen one. It was considered an antiquated way to use magic. Evidently it was also efficient.

I landed on the cool floor with all the elegance of a brick and knocked the stone out of the panel with a flick of my claw. It rolled out and clattered onto the tiles where it lay still, barely a metre from the wall.

Was that far enough to stop it from working?

I had just finished that thought when a wave of energy washed over me. It felt like hot wind that made my skin tingle. I fell to my knees, suddenly groggy, but not like when I had been tranquillised. This was something different altogether, something much more powerful.

I felt as if the stone was absorbing every bit of magic inside me, witch and shifter. I was vaguely aware of returning to witch form before I slumped down on the cold, hard floor.

I WOKE BRIEFLY.

I wasn't sure what woke me until I heard voices nearby.

"…damaged the stone."

"…she's going to be furious."

"…have our heads."

"I'll handle her."

She who?

I opened my eyes a crack. As far as I could tell, I hadn't moved from where I'd fallen. I was very aware I was now fully naked. Fitz was dead, so I didn't need to worry about him, but that didn't mean I was safe.

I wriggled my fingers and toes. Could I shift again if I needed to?

The stone. I should be able to use magic now. Unless…the sensation of the stone sucking it away had actually done that.

Before I could try, the speakers stepped closer. One bent down and picked up the stone in a black bag.

"Don't touch it." A voice spoke from behind me.

"Of course not, love. I'm no fool." The man with the bag closed the top of it and turned so I caught a look at his face.

What the fuck?

His skin was red. Not flushed like a blush or

sunburn, but red like… Nothing I had ever seen. Narrow eyes, like slits shone with an orange glow.

Part of me wanted to get up and run like hells. I wasn't sure if he knew I was watching, but I sensed he did. For some reason, he didn't see me as a threat.

Shame I can't say the same for you, buddy.

He stepped around me and headed toward the door with his companions. I wanted to see if they were like him, but I dared not roll over to find out. I preferred not threatening and alive to satisfying my curiosity. For once.

The door clicked shut and the darkness claimed me again.

"PEYTON? Hey, come on, wake up. Shit, do you think she's hurt? I can't see any sign of injury. Peyton?"

I groaned. Once again, my head pounded. Great. This day sucked.

"She's alive!"

"Stop shouting, Dyson." I peered up at him. "I love you, too. Why aren't you wearing a shirt?"

He smiled, but it faded quickly. "I had to shift. We dealt with an agent or two. We need to get out of here."

"Right." I sat up and winced. "Are you all right?" I gave him a speculative look.

"I'm drug free," he said firmly. "Corinne gave me an antidote."

I nodded. I'd have to remember to thank her later. "Say, did you see a redhead go past?"

"Fitz is gone, remember?" Blake stepped into view. His eyes widened as he saw me naked. He promptly took off his agent jacket and draped it over me.

Aww, I guess chivalry isn't dead after all.

"Thanks." I pulled it closer. "I don't mean red hair, I mean…" Maybe I had imagined it. I looked over to where the stone had lain. It was gone now.

"What was that?" I let Dyson help me to my feet and took a moment to admire his dick. Hey, I wasn't dead. "The stone. It was here…"

Corinne glanced around before exchanging looks and shrugs with Blake. "Rumour says the dampening field was created by an ancient artefact." Her blonde hair was messy and flecked with blood. "If my grandmother was to be believed, it was crafted by demons."

"Demons?" I laughed awkwardly. "There's no such things as demons." Or was there? Gods, I didn't know anymore. Redhead certainly looked—well—

demonic, even if he hadn't harmed me in any way. Not that I knew of. I hadn't become his lunch at any rate.

"Come on, we need to hurry. Once the field dropped, a bunch of witches started to fight back, but they won't be distracted for long." Corinne led the way to the door and peered out.

"Um, wouldn't it be easier to fly out?" I asked.

"Can you carry us all?" Dyson asked.

I blinked at him. "Stairs it is then."

"This is all too familiar," Dyson remarked as we headed for the door to emergency stairs.

"Isn't it though?" I grimaced. All we were lacking was Matt, also naked or in gargoyle form. "We really have to stop Zeta from chasing us around places with multiple floors."

"Agreed. Stairs are so claustrophobic. A fire-fighter pole would be good right now."

"Or a…wait." I pulled him back into the room and gestured for the others to follow. "Has anyone got a phone?"

"I do." Blake unlocked his and handed it to me.

I opened the magic app.

"Oh no, please say you're not," Dyson groaned. A smile tugged at the corners of his mouth.

"Oh, I most certainly am." I grinned. I walked to

the window and aimed the phone. The magic came rushing to me faster than ever. Maybe the stone had had some kind of impact on me. I couldn't think about that right now. I focused, clicked on the screen and watched the magic come to life.

"Other people might be cool," I handed Blake back his phone with a flourish, "but they're not "escaping from an evil organisation's secret compound by gigantic, magical waterslide" cool."

"You're fucking crazy," Dyson told me. 'And I love it. Now, let's get out of here."

I climbed out the window and onto the top of the slide. It was still a long way down and I was held up by nothing but magic, but I sat in the flow of water and let gravity take me toward the ground in a blur.

Wheeee.

25

I slid out into a pair of arms. As we fell in a tangle of legs and confusion, I thought I must have bowled down a Zeta agent.

I drew magic, ready to blast them back.

"Woah, steady there, loveliness." Nash raised his hands in surrender. He was wet from where I ran into him, but apparently unharmed.

"What the hells?" I pushed myself to my knees. It was good to see him. So good my heart skipped a beat. "It's about time you showed up."

He frowned.

"Sir," I added.

He smiled. "It took a while to find where they'd taken you. I—" He grabbed my hand and rolled us both to one side just as Dyson slid out of the end of the slide.

"Maybe we should find somewhere safer to talk," I remarked.

"This works for me."

Of course it did, I was lying on top of him, his arms around me.

"Save it for when we're not outside a building full of Zeta agents," Matt suggested.

I glanced over. I hadn't seen him until now. "He has a point."

"I always do," Matt replied. He drew back as Corinne landed neatly on her feet.

"She's with us." I got to my feet but held on to Nash's hand. I wasn't ready to be apart from him yet. He felt like…safety. "Him, too."

Blake slid out a moment later, uniform drenched, huge smile on his face. He looked like a little boy who had just discovered adrenaline hits.

The waterslide disappeared a moment later.

We followed suit, just as a pair of agents appeared in the window we had used to escape. They peered around, spoke words I couldn't hear, then disappeared back inside.

"They'll be down here before long," Nash said softly. "Everyone head north. We'll meet at the car."

"Roger that," Matt replied. I hadn't seen him take Dyson's hand, but he must have. Good, he would be safe with Matt.

Nash squeezed my hand and we started walking.

"I guess you guys took out any alarms on the perimeter fence," I said conversationally.

"Alarms and guards," Nash replied in a tone which suggested he'd killed or at least maimed them.

He would be in a dark mood later, but I wouldn't let him be alone to brood.

"Are you all right?" he asked softly.

I took a moment to respond. "Physically I am. The rest will take a while." I gave him a brief rundown of what had taken place, including what they'd said about my mother, my father ,and the UA.

"Did you know the University of Arcana was run by Zeta?" I asked. "I guess the horrid uniforms they made us wear should have been an indication. I mean, who would make us wear those unless they were evil?"

Nash mouth quirked upward, but he didn't look surprised. He chewed his lip and led me toward a copse of trees. "I was starting to suspect as much. They knew how to reach you and Dyson. We surmised that someone had told them, but I wondered if there was more to it than that. The pink donut wasn't so much an infiltration as it was an experiment."

"One Kane inadvertently took part in with his work in the lab." I sighed. "Where is he anyway? And Ariana and Hamish? They won't be safe there anymore."

"Right." Nash pulled out his phone, punched in some text with one deft thumb and slid it back in his pocket.

I waited for a moment but when he didn't say anything else, I asked, "And?"

"And what?"

"Will they be okay?"

"My priority is to get you somewhere safer—"

"Lincoln Nash." I stopped mid-step.

He frowned at my use of his full name. Or the name he went by, at least. I was almost certain it wasn't his real name.

"You know I can't rest until I know they're safe too."

He sighed and tugged me onward. "Shhh." He looked back over his shoulder.

"Don't—" Then I heard them. Shouts and the baying of dogs.

"Shit. I don't want to kill any dogs," I whispered. "That's bad juju."

"Assuming they're actually dogs," Nash replied.

"Oh." I froze.

Heads appeared, bounding over the terrain we'd just crossed. Three heads. One body.

Cerberus. Trust Zeta to have an actual fucking hellhound!

"What do we do?" I asked frantically. My phoenix form could probably rip the hound's heads off, but that was if I could shift and was willing to kill again. Which I wasn't if I could help it.

Cerberus stopped and bared three sets of teeth and a whole bunch of saliva. He growled deep in the back of all of his throats. He definitely meant business.

He stalked forward.

"What else are you going to fight a dog with?" Nash asked. How did he sound so calm?

"Uh." It took me a moment. "Right."

"On three. One. Two. Three."

He dropped the magic bubble from around us just as I conjured the tiger from my tattoo. Was it bigger than the last time? It certainly seemed more solid somehow. I suppose I was getting better at conjuring.

Cerberus skidded to a halt in front of the tiger.

"Now, we run." Nash snapped the bubble back

around us, took my hand and we bolted as the sound of two large animals clashing rang out.

A canine howl of pain made me wince, especially when it was cut short.

"One head down, two to go." Nash sounded grim.

I grimaced and kept running, even though the ground was tearing up my bare feet.

"Not much further," he told me. "Can you climb?" He waved toward a wire fence as we rounded some trees.

"Just try to stop me," I replied. I released his hand as I drew to make a bubble around myself. The magic felt as though it flew into me. I caught a look of surprise on Nash's face before our bubbles separated.

I didn't take time to think about it, I just scaled the fence. My small feet fit nicely into the holes and over the top. I dropped to the ground just as the fence started to buzz.

"It looks like they got the power back on," Nash remarked. "Hopefully the others got over in time."

"Yeah." I glanced around but saw no sign of them and no indication any guards had seen a naked shifter climbing the fence. I could only hope they'd make it to our meeting point.

"I'm right beside you," Nash said.

I felt a hand brush my chest. I dropped my bubble for just long enough for Nash's to envelope me again.

"Hey," he said softly. "I think I forgot to mention I'm glad you're alive." His lips brushed mine and sent a jolt of heat through me. "Come on, let's get somewhere safer."

"Good plan," I replied, although part of me wanted to tear off his damp clothes and let him take me up against a tree. More than that though, I didn't want to get caught. My libido would have to wait.

Breathless, we trotted the rest of the way to a small SUV parked amongst the bushes maybe a kilometre from the Zeta building.

To my relief, Matt and Dyson were already sitting inside, Dyson wearing a blanket. Blake and Corinne trotted up shortly afterward.

"We can't go with you," Corinne said. "We need to report to the council. They'll need to know what happened here. They may also reconsider recommending the UA to young paranormals."

"Good idea," I said dryly. They would still go there, though. The education they got at the university was second to none. Well, except the Academy of Modern Magic. And maybe the College of Advanced Magical Education.

"We did good here today," Blake assured me. "You especially. A lot of witches owe you a debt of gratitude."

"Thanks," I said awkwardly. Some wouldn't though; those who thought they were doing a good thing.

"I'm sure I'll see you again." He gave me a dimpled smile and a kiss on the cheek before the pair clasped hands and disappeared.

"Yeah," I said softly. "I'm sure."

"Hey." Dyson climbed out of the SUV. "Kane called. He said Ariana had insisted he go with her and Hamish to the city for lunch. Then she told him why he can't go back."

I glanced at Nash, who shrugged as if he wasn't behind all of that.

"I guess we'll meet them there."

"There's a little matter of all our belongings," Matt said, as if this was all my fault.

"Don't worry about that," I said, "Xav owes me a favour. I bet he'll be thrilled to pack up everything we own and ship it off to…wherever we're going."

"The council will find a place," Nash assured me. "At least we don't have to hide anymore." He pulled me to him and kissed me deeply. He slipped his hands under the jacket and cupped my rear.

"I guess I'm driving," Matt remarked.

"You guessed right." Nash guided me to the back of the car and closed the door behind us.

I vaguely heard the front doors close as Dyson and Matt got in.

Nash eased off the jacket I had been wearing and kissed my neck. Slowly, he moved down my body. He teased my nipple with the tip of his tongue and slipped a hand down between my legs.

I parted them for him.

"Shouldn't you two have seatbelts on?" Matt asked dryly.

"Drive carefully," Nash growled. He dipped two fingers inside me. I was already as wet as hells.

I moaned softly. And again when we stopped at a set of traffic lights and a truck pulled up alongside us. The driver peered down at us. His eyes widened as I unzipped Nash's pants and freed his erection. I ran my hand up and down his hot length.

I gave the truck driver a smile and closed my eyes. I rocked my body against Nash's touch. My lips dropped apart and I panted as I came.

The truck drew away a moment later.

"You're so beautiful." Nash carefully moved himself up the car seat until he lay over me. I wound my legs around him.

"Even when I'm not tied up, sir?" I teased.

"Even then." He slid his cock into me and groaned.

I sighed with the pleasure of him filling me fully. I opened my eyes a crack to see Dyson watching from the front seat. He gave me a smile. Someday I wanted to have him inside me. If I was honest, I wanted Matt too. I almost insisted we pull over so they could join us in the back, but there would be time for that later. That didn't stop me from picturing them pushing back the seats and lying beside us. I imagined taking Matt's cock into my mouth, while my fingers curled around Dyson's. Then Kane was there in my mind, his fingertip teasing my rear hole.

Nash pulled almost all the way out and slid back into me. He went still, then drew back again.

"Peyton," he said, his mouth beside my ear. "I'm falling so hard for you."

I swallowed. "I'm falling for you too, sir."

Gods, what was I going to do with all of these guys and my feelings for them all? Part of me was even eager to see Blake again. I was certainly looking forward to seeing Kane, safe and sound.

Nash grunted and moved faster. Every thrust drove me closer and closer to the edge.

"Say that again," he said, breathlessly.

"Sir," I said. "Fuck me harder, sir."

He grunted and came, spilling hot seed into me and driving me over the edge again. I arched my back as pleasure washed over me.

"Gods, yes…sir."

I had barely started to come down before he relaxed his weight on top of me and sighed.

"You're amazing, but they won't stop hunting us," he said softly. "We got away, but this isn't over."

I closed my eyes to keep from looking out of the car. If someone was following, I didn't want to see them, not yet.

***

Will the AMM find a new home? Who is the guy with the red face? Will Blake return? Find out in book 3, Logical Magic.

ABOUT THE AUTHOR

Maggie Alabaster is the reverse harem and fantasy romance author.

She lives in NSW, Australia with one spouse, two daughters, dog, cat, rabbits and countless birds.

Sign up for my newsletter! Sign Up!
Join my reader group! Join here!
Follow me on Bookbub! Click here to follow me!

Summer's Harem

Book 1: Shimmer

Book 2: Glimmer

Book 3: Flicker

Complete collection

Short reads

Taken by the Snowmen

Jingle All the Way

Also by Maggie Alabaster and Erin Yoshikawa

Caught by the Tide

Book 1–Pursued by Shadows

Book 2 Pursued by Darkness

Book 3 Pursued by Monsters